TOMATO BASIL MURDER

THE DARLING DELI SERIES, BOOK 7

PATTI BENNING

SUMMER PRESCOTT BOOKS PUBLISHING

CHAPTER ONE

"Are you sure you're going to be okay until Darrin gets here?" Moira Darling asked Meg Brownell, her most recent hire. The young woman nodded, her bobbed hair bouncing.

"I'll be fine, Ms. D. It's only an hour, and we haven't been that busy today," she replied, enthusiastic as ever. "You go ahead and help Candice. The deli will be in good hands."

Moira knew her employee was more than capable of handling any routine issues that might come up, but she was always reluctant to leave the deli when her assistant manager Darrin wasn't there. Darling's DELIcious Delights was her pride and joy; the little deli was proof to her that even a middle-aged woman like herself could still start something new and make a difference in the world, no matter how small. It was her pride and joy and, other than the raising of her twenty-year-old daughter, the greatest accomplishment of her life so far.

Candice, about to embark on a business venture of her own, had asked Moira to visit her in Lake Marion to go over the final renovation plans for the toy store that would soon be her daughter's candy shop. *The deli will be fine,* Moira told herself. *Meg is smart; she can manage it on her own for an hour. Give the girl some credit.*

"All right," she said at last. "I know you'll do fine. Don't hesitate to call me if you need anything, though."

"I won't, Ms. D. Have a nice day. Tell Candice 'hi' for me." Meg waved her boss out the door with a smile.

After a quick pit stop at her small apartment on the outskirts of town to get Maverick, her German shepherd, she was on her way. Lake Marion was a scenic twenty-minute drive away from her hometown of Maple Creek, and Moira had traveled the distance so often in the last few months that sometimes she thought she could do it in her sleep.

Out of habit, she grabbed her phone to call her sort-of boyfriend, David Morris, to see if he could meet her for lunch. Just before she pressed the speed dial button, she remembered that he was out of town. The handsome private investigator was at a conference in Maryland until next Monday, so until then, she was on her own.

When the familiar blue crescent of the town's namesake lake appeared through the trees, she knew she was close. Easing off on the gas as she entered the town limits, she unrolled the passenger window for Maverick, who happily stuck his head out, long pink tongue lolling in the wind. She had adopted the German shepherd only a few months ago, when his previous owner had been arrested for murder. The dog had fit into her life seamlessly, and she would forever be thankful that a fireman had saved him from the fire that had destroyed her house the month before.

Living in the apartment wasn't terrible; her neighbors were friendly and one of them had even become a regular at the deli after discovering that Moira owned it. However, the tiny living space was a far cry from the gorgeous house that she had lived in for over twenty years. Sometimes she still woke up in her small, dark bedroom wondering where she was, the fire and subsequent move nothing but a nightmare for a few wonderful moments. Then she remembered everything that had been lost in the house fire, and her tears welled up again.

It was hard to be unhappy right now, however. The day was beautiful, and as she pulled into the small parking lot behind Candice's store, she found herself looking forward to spending the next few hours with her daughter. The twenty-year-old had lived with Moira until recently, and she often found herself missing her daughter's constant company.

She let herself in the old toy store's back door, which was propped open, and made her way through to the open front room, Maverick racing eagerly ahead of her. The room was empty; even the shelves were gone, the walls bare as Candice prepared the store to be repainted. The huge picture window at the front of the store was stripped of the signs and posters that had accumulated on it during the toy store's long life, and now let in a generous amount of sunlight. Located right at the center of the small town, on Main Street, the store was sure to get a lot of business—or so Moira and Candice hoped.

"Thanks for coming, Mom," Candice said. She was sitting on a folding chair at the counter, her blonde hair pulled back in a messy bun. "They want to start installing the floors next week, so I have to be completely sure of what I want. It's harder to decide than I thought it would be."

"Well, let's see what you've got to choose from," Moira said, unfolding a second chair and setting it up next to her daughter. "You'll probably want something pretty hardy, since you'll have a lot of children in your store. I'm surprised this wood held up for as long as it did." She gazed across the worn flooring of the toy store. It badly needed re-staining, and parts of it had water damage. She had to agree with her daughter that completely new flooring would look best and, as long as they chose something other than wood, would require less upkeep in the long run.

They eventually settled on a light-colored laminate that looked like wood but would be much easier to clean and take care of. As Candice described her plans for painting and installing new shelves, Moira smiled and thought back to her exciting first days of making plans for the deli. Like Candice, she had taken over a store that was going out of business. In her case, the owner of the bakery had been more than happy to give her a deal on some of the appliances as well, which had been a blessing for the just-starting-out deli owner. Candice would have to purchase her own new appliances, but the small business loan would cover nearly everything.

"Have you thought of a name for the store yet?" Moira asked, idly flipping through a catalog advertising custom paper and plastic bags, trays, and even molds. *Maybe I should order some for the deli*, she thought.

"Not yet." Her daughter sighed. "That's another thing I'll have to make a decision about. I don't know how I'll do it without second-guessing myself."

"Just go with your gut," Moira told her with a smile. "I'm sure whatever you choose will be perfect."

"I hope so. I'm excited about this, Mom, but it's all so stressful."

"I have an idea," her mother replied, looking out the window at the gorgeous day with clear blue skies. "Let's go to the beach this weekend for a mother-daughter day of de-stressing. I have Sunday off."

"Oh." Candice bit her lip. "Um, actually, Dad is coming to visit, and I was going to spend the weekend hanging out with him. Didn't he tell you?"

"No. He hasn't said anything." She frowned. Her ex-husband lived on the other side of the country, and rarely came to visit. She hadn't seen him in years, and wasn't sure she needed to now.

"Oh, well, he should be here Friday, and he's staying until Sunday evening. Maybe we can all go out to dinner or something," her daughter said, a hopeful glint in her eye.

"Maybe," Moira said reluctantly. She knew her daughter still entertained dreams of her parents getting back together, and she didn't want to encourage any false hopes. "I'll have to check my schedule." She sighed and looked out the window again. Somehow the sunny day didn't look so bright anymore.

She drove the long way home after leaving Candice's store that afternoon. She wouldn't be needed at the deli, and she didn't want to spend the rest of the evening sitting around her tiny apartment. A glance at the clock told her it was a bit late to go to the lake; there would only be about an hour of good sun left, and after she stopped at home to get her bathing suit, a couple of towels, and Maverick's long leash, there would hardly be any time at all. *A scenic drive will have to do*, she told herself.

As she drove, she couldn't help but think of the conversation she and her daughter had had earlier. Mike was coming to Maple Creek. She hadn't seen him since Candice's high school graduation—had it really been three years? *Does he know about the house?* she wondered. Candice had certainly told him, though Moira knew that the responsibility should have fallen on her own shoulders. She really should have called him weeks ago to tell him about the fire. Though his name was no longer on the deed, it had been their house for nearly ten years.

Shaking her head, wishing she could snap out of her introspective mood, Moira eased her car around a tight curve. She was going slowly enough to catch sight of the For Sale sign partly hidden behind the branches of an enthusiastic bush. Her curiosity piqued, she allowed the car to slow to a stop on the gravel shoulder.

Moving the branches aside, she saw the sign had a street address and phone number written on it in permanent marker along with Maple Creek Realty's logo. She looked around until she spotted a mailbox just past her car with a matching address. *A house for sale out here, huh?* she thought. *It is a nice area...* The woods between Lake Marion and Maple Creek were thick, and on this road most houses were far enough back that you couldn't even see them through the trees.

I'm not ready to buy a new house yet, she told herself. *And even if I was, I probably couldn't afford to get one in such a nice area.* Even though she knew it would be best just to get back in the car and drive on, she couldn't help but keep staring at the sign she had almost missed. She didn't necessarily believe in fate, but it couldn't hurt to look.

She drove slowly up the gravel driveway, planning on just getting close enough to get a look at the house before leaving. She wasn't prepared for the gorgeous two-story stone house that appeared when she rounded a curve, and she felt an immediate desire to start figuring out what it would take to buy it.

The house was nestled in a small clearing, surrounded by trees. There was a large garden currently in bloom with a multitude of flowers, some of which Moira couldn't even name. Maverick, who had his entire head hanging out the window in an effort to see what their unplanned stop was all about, barked at a black squirrel that was busily foraging on the forest floor. The air was a few degrees cooler under the canopy, and the shade rippled as the leaves far above danced in the wind. It was beautiful. *I would love to live here*, she thought. *I would love to call this place home.*

CHAPTER TWO

"Is this the one?" Madeline Frau asked, turning her computer so Moira could see the screen. "It's the only one I can find on Morel Street."

"Yes, that's it." She gazed at the photo of the beautiful stone house, then glanced at the price and sighed. She doubted she would be able to afford it, not after cosigning the small business loan for Candice.

"Would you like to set up a showing?" the realtor asked. "The seller just lowered the price, so it would probably be smart to move quickly. I've got a feeling that this house won't be on the market for much longer."

"I'm not sure." Moira hesitated, not wanting to waste the time of the pleasant woman who sat across from her. She did want to see the house, but wasn't sure she would be able to find a way to afford it, even with how well the deli was doing right now.

"Taking a look won't hurt," the other woman said with an understanding smile. Her eyes flickered with sudden recognition. "Say, aren't you the woman that owns the deli across town?"

"That's me." It always surprised her when someone recognized her from the deli, though she loved knowing that so many people enjoyed the fresh, healthy foods she sold. "Moira Darling, owner of Darling's DELIcious Delights."

"Well, let's see what we can do for you. We can start with you seeing the inside of the house and a tour of the property, and if you like it we can go from there. I heard about your house burning down. I'm very sorry about that."

"Thanks. I wish the insurance company would hurry up and finish their investigation. I guess it's taking them a lot longer than usual, since the police determined the fire to be arson." She knew the man who set the fire had been the same one who had kidnapped her a few weeks before, but he was already being investigated for multiple felonies; she doubted that her house fire was high on the priority list of any investigator, not when the man was facing murder charges.

"I'm sure you'll get the insurance money soon enough," Madeline assured her. "And when you do, wouldn't it be great to have a perfect house to spend it on?"

Unable to resist the other woman's optimism, Moira agreed to meet her at the stone house on Sunday. She wished that David would be back by then, but if she liked it she could always see it again with him along. She'd want Candice to get a chance to look at the house too, but since her daughter was planning on spending all day Sunday with her father, that would have to wait.

Thinking of her ex, she realized that he was supposed to arrive in Maple Creek in just a few hours. Candice was meeting him for dinner, and David wouldn't be back from his trip for a few more days, so it looked like she was on her own tonight. *Unless I want to call Denise or Martha,* she thought. *Maybe we could grab dinner at the Grill.* The Redwood

Grill was the wonderful steakhouse that Denise owned. *That actually sounds like a great idea. I could use some time out with my friends.*

A few hours later, she slid into the booth at her regular table across from Denise. The Grill was busy, as it was most Friday nights, but the other woman's highly efficient staff made sure things were running smoothly.

"How are you?" she asked her friend. "It's been a while." Since her house had burned down, Moira hadn't had much time for social visits.

"Oh, I'm been fine. Busy, you know," the tall redheaded woman replied. "I'm glad we both had time for this. Did Martha say when she would be here?"

"She shouldn't be much longer. She told me her book club got done at seven, and she would head over right after."

"I hope she doesn't mind if we order an appetizer without her—I'm starved," Denise admitted. "You'd think that working in a restaurant, I'd never go hungry, but my hostess for the first shift called in sick and I covered for her. Between that and checking in on our new chef, I haven't had time for more than a quick bite since we opened this morning."

"I know how it is," Moira assured her. "When you're the boss, sometimes you've got to do everyone's job all at once." She took a sip of her water, then added, "Tell me about your new chef. Did Lorenzo leave?"

"No, he just asked for a reduction in hours," the other woman explained. "His wife just had a baby, and he wanted to be home more. The new chef's name is Annalise, and she just got out of culinary school. She has phenomenal references, though, and even though she's relatively inexperienced, she has yet to make a dish that's anything other than mouthwatering. Don't tell her I said that though, one thing she doesn't need is more strokes for her ego."

"Hearing your stories always makes me glad my deli is on the small side," Moira admitted. "I'm not sure I would be able to organize as many people as you do or deal with so many conflicting personalities. I love the fact that my employees are really more like family."

"Well, sometimes *I* envy *you*. I wish my employees cared about the Grill as much as yours care about the deli. While most of them are hardworking, they're in it for the paycheck. Lorenzo and Annalise are the only ones that truly seem passionate about their work, and sometimes that passion does more harm than good." Denise sighed and drained the last of her water, then waved a young waitress over to take their appetizer orders.

By the time Martha joined them, the two friends were digging into the blooming onion and guacamole and chips they had ordered to tide themselves over. Just a few weeks ago, Moira might have opted for a salad or another healthy option, but the stress of losing the house and worrying about Candice seemed to have sucked away a few extra pounds. *One unhealthy meal with my friends won't hurt my waistline any,* she decided.

"What is *that?*" Martha asked as she sat down, staring at the blooming onion.

"An onion, dipped in sweet garlic batter and deep fried," Denise said. She grinned. "Otherwise known as a heart attack waiting to happen, but what's the fun if you never live a little?"

Martha, a stick-thin woman with mousy brown hair, gave the dish a dubious glance as she sat down next to Moira. With her brother in jail and her sister dead, she had lost more in the past year than even Moira had, and she admired her friend for managing to keep her life together despite everything she had been through. *None of us are the type to give up easily*, she thought, gazing fondly at her two closest girlfriends.

"So, what's new in your life, Moira?" Denise asked once Martha had gotten settled. "Have you settled into that apartment yet?"

"I don't think it will ever feel like home," she replied. "But at least it's a place to call my own. I'm glad that I don't have to impose on Candice any longer."

"Speaking of Candice, how is her candy shop coming along?"

"She's been working really hard to get it ready." Moira told them. "She's got everything left over from the toy store torn out, and is just about ready to have new flooring installed. She does need some help coming up with a name, however, so if either of you have any good ideas, I can pass them on."

"It looks like we could just tell Candice ourselves," Martha said, nodding towards the front of the restaurant.

Moira spun around to see her daughter talking with the hostess. Standing a few feet behind her was Mike Thomson, her ex-husband and Candice's father. He looked the nearly same as he had years ago, other than the fact that his skin was darker, tanned by the California sun, and his blond hair had been shaved down from the thick locks that she remembered to a short, nearly military cut. *Maybe he started going bald,* she thought, amused by the prospect.

Mentally berating herself for not guessing that this was there her daughter would choose to go out to eat with her father, she turned back to her friends. She hadn't told them that Mike was coming back to town yet, and it looked like she had put it off for long enough.

"I didn't know she was going to be here," she admitted with a sigh. "She's spending the evening with her dad."

"Oh, that's Mike?" Martha asked. She had met him a few times when her older sister Emilia used to babysit Candice. "I didn't recognize him with the haircut."

"Your ex?" Denise asked. "Does he visit often?"

"No, this is the first time he's seen Candice since she graduated from high school," Moira replied. "I'm glad for her sake that he decided to fly out, but I would rather avoid him. Too many bad memories."

"What does David think of Mike being around?" Martha asked, raising her eyebrows.

"Well... I haven't told him," she admitted. "Candice just told me he was coming this afternoon. David won't be back until after Mike leaves, anyway."

"Do you think he'd be worried about you spending time with your ex?" her friend asked.

"David isn't the jealous type." Moira considered for a moment. "Mike is, but he has a girlfriend out in California, according to Candice. I doubt he would care either, if he knew about David."

"They're coming this way," Denise said. "I hope Ashley doesn't seat them next to us."

Luckily, Candice, Mike, and the waitress walked right by them without a glance. Candice was too busy talking with her father to notice the three women, for which Moira was grateful. Now if she could just get through the rest of the dinner without being forced to somehow find the energy to talk with her ex-husband, her weekend would be off to a good start.

CHAPTER THREE

She managed to avoid her ex-husband only until breakfast the next day, when he walked straight into the deli while she was chatting with a customer at the register. The fact that Candice wasn't with him meant that he was there for only one reason: to talk to her.

"I'm amazed by what you've accomplished," he said once she had finished ringing up the customer. "It's a cute place." He leaned against the counter, the sleeve of his shirt riding up to casually expose a fancy gold wristwatch. *It looks like he finally found the success that he wanted*, she thought. What must he think of her, still living in the same town in a tiny apartment?

"Thanks," she said grudgingly. "How's life out west?"

"Fun." He grinned. "I haven't even seen snow since I moved out there. Southern California has the best weather."

"I think I would miss not having all four seasons like we do here." She didn't know if she was trying to convince him or herself more. One of the points of contention in their marriage had always been her reluctance to move away from her home state. While it was true that she couldn't imagine living somewhere it didn't snow, she couldn't help but think it would be nice not to have to deal with below zero temperatures and five-foot-deep snow drifts for three or more months out of the year.

"Candice said the same thing," he told her. "I admit I was disappointed when she told me she was going to start a business around here, instead of moving out to Cali with me. But then, she always did take more after you."

Moira pressed her lips together, resisting the urge to point out that if he had actually been around for the better part of Candice's childhood, then she might have taken more after him. All of the self-help books that she had read had said that it was best for children if estranged parents maintained a good relationship. Sometimes it wasn't easy to stay civil, but she was determined to do what was best for Candice.

"How is your girlfriend doing?" she asked instead, trying to move the conversation away from their shared past.

"We broke up," he said, shrugging. "I thought it would be a good time to travel—get out of Cali, revisit the past a bit. Catch up with Candice."

"Well, it's nice that she gets to spend some time with you. I know she's missed you these last few years."

"I meant to fly back for a few days last summer, but I just had too much to do at work." He shook his head. "I'm honestly amazed what my little girl has accomplished. I'm going to try to find the time to visit again in a few months, once her candy shop is up and running. Remember when she wanted to be a fire-fighter?"

"I remember," Moira said, unable to help a smile. "She loved putting out the bonfire we had every year on the first day of summer. I have to say, I'm glad she's pursuing a different path. I don't know how I'd stand it if she had such a dangerous career." She sobered as she remembered the inferno that had engulfed her house. She was grateful that her daughter would be running a business instead of putting her life on the line to put out fires. *Not that being a business owner is always much safer,* she thought, thinking of her own adventures over the past few months. Hopefully Candice wouldn't have quite such an eventful experience with her own store.

"I'm sorry about the house," her ex-husband said, watching her face carefully. She was always surprised at how well he could read her, even after being divorced for a decade. "I was completely stunned when Candice told me. I'm glad you're both all right."

"Thanks. We were both lucky. Even my dog is okay." Moira attempted a smile. "If you get a chance, feel free to drive by and take a look at what's left of it. The investigation is ongoing, but when they finish up I'm thinking of selling it. The damage is bad enough that I'd have to rebuild the entire house, and it just wouldn't be the same."

"I'll swing by when I leave here," he said. "Take care, Moira." Glancing around once more at her deli, he lifted his arm in a wave goodbye and left. Moira stood at the register for a moment, surprised by how well their conversation had gone. Then she glanced at the clock and, realizing the time, headed back into the kitchen to get started on the day's special.

Starting with a tomato sauce base, she added vegetable broth, a few diced garlic cloves, and a splash of olive oil to the pot, then turned the burner to medium. While the soup base heated, she pulled a bundle of fresh baby spinach leaves out of the vegetable crisper drawer in the fridge and began to chop them roughly. Once she had a few cups ready to go, she dumped it into the base, which was now simmering. She knew from experience the spinach wouldn't take long to cook, so she hurried to add the cheese and mushroom-stuffed tortellini, which had been handmade by a local farmer. Within minutes, the soup was simmering away and Moira's work was nearly done. It was a simple and quick recipe that was also mouth-wateringly good. Topped with shredded white cheddar cheese and paired with a toasted cheddar and tomato sandwich with fresh spinach leaves, it made a hearty and delicious meal.

"Wow, Ms. Darling, whatever you're making smells amazing," Dante said a few minutes later poking his head into the kitchen just as she was finishing up slicing the locally grown, organic tomatoes for the sandwiches. "When will it be ready? There's a customer waiting at the register. He wants to know if he should wait or come back later."

"The soup should be ready in just a few minutes," she told him, peering into the pot. "As soon as the tortellini starts floating, I can serve it."

When the soup was ready, she ladled it into a bowl herself and brought a tray out for the elderly man that was waiting so patiently. She smiled as she watched him make his way over to one of the bistro tables and dig in. No matter how many times a day she saw someone eating her food, it still warmed her heart to watch them enjoy it. *I've always loved cooking*, she thought. *Now I get to do it every day, for the whole town.*

Lost in her thoughts, she didn't look up when the deli's front door opened and someone walked in. It wasn't until she saw the shadow fall across her register that she glanced up and saw Martha's amused face smiling at her.

"I'm so sorry," Moira exclaimed, jumping slightly. "I was busy thinking."

"About you-know-who?" Martha asked, her eyes sparkling. "I was going to stop in earlier, but I saw him in here."

"I was actually thinking about how much I love my job," she replied with a smile. She guessed that Martha was secretly wondering if she was still attracted to her ex-husband. In truth, David was the only man who crossed her mind these days. "My *ex* and I had a perfectly civil conversation, though. I am glad he stopped by. At least he got a chance to see what I've accomplished with my life so far." She couldn't help but feel proud that she had managed not only to raise Candice as a single mom, but also to start a thriving business, all on her own.

"Good for you, showing him how well you're doing," her friend said. She turned, and Moira noticed for the first time a petite blonde woman behind her. "Sorry, I've been rude. This is Beverly. She's my first guest. I'm just showing her around town, and thought it might be nice to stop in and introduce her to you."

"Oh, it's very nice to meet you, Beverly," Moira said, reaching out to shake her hand. She had known that Martha was planning on renting out rooms in her sister Emilia's old house, and possibly even starting up a bed and breakfast at some point, but she was surprised that her friend had found her first guest so quickly. "How long are you in town for?"

"Just a few days," Beverly replied. "I flew in to check up on my boyfriend. I think he's been seeing another woman. In fact, I just confirmed it." She pursed her lips, then smiled over at Martha. "Even though this isn't turning out to be the happiest trip in the world, staying at that gorgeous house is just so much better than staying at one of those terrible little motels on the highway. I'm so glad I found your advertisement online."

"And I'm happy my first guest turned out to be so pleasant," Martha said, returning the smile. "I've been nervous about opening my doors up to strangers, but the house just feels too empty when I'm there alone."

"You're braver than I would be," Moira told her. "I've met some pretty frightening people in the past few months. I don't think I'd be comfortable sharing a house with a stranger. No offense," she added quickly, turning to Beverly. "You just never know what someone is really like until it's too late."

"That's very true," Beverly said. "You never really know what someone is like on the inside."

"I think it's safe to say we've all made the mistake of trusting someone we shouldn't have," the deli owner said. "All we can do is move on."

"Too true," Martha said. Her eyes wandered over to the blackboard where the day's special was written, and her gaze brightened. "Tortellini and spinach soup? That sounds delicious. Can I have one of the combos?"

"Of course. Would you like anything, Beverly?"

"Oh, well, I really should watch my weight..." She trailed off, clearly mentally debating with herself. "Do you have salads?"

"We sure do," Moira told her. "We can make just about anything you want. What are you in the mood for?"

"Can you make a salad with kale, arugula, and spinach leaves, topped with blue cheese crumbles, dried cranberries, crushed walnuts, and some sort of vinaigrette dressing?"

"I think we've got all of that. Give me just a second—I'll go get our food. If it's okay, I'll join you—I haven't eaten since about seven this morning," she told them.

"Of course," Beverly said. "And no hurry, I'm completely free until later tonight. It's wonderful to have a chance to tour such a quaint town."

Quaint, Moira thought, amused, as she ducked into the kitchen to get their food. *She should see some of the places farther north.* It was obvious the blonde woman was used to living in a much more sophisticated urban environment. *I hope she enjoys what's left of her vacation. It's good to spend some time away from the city. We could all use a break from the hustle and bustle of our busy lives once in a while.*

CHAPTER FOUR

Her early morning routine with Maverick had changed substantially since they had moved into the apartment. There weren't anymore long, leisurely walks down quiet residential streets since the apartment bordered a busy road and she always seemed to start the dog's walk just in time for rush hour. Instead, she opted for a quick jog around the apartment complex, which was at least enough to get her heart rate up and to get the dog panting.

This morning was no different from all the others; they jogged from her apartment door all the way to the office on the other side of the complex, where she said good morning to the woman working the desk and Maverick got his daily treat and pats from the staff. The sharp chlorine scent of the indoor pool filled her nostrils, and Moira promised herself that she would check it out soon. *As soon as I have time,* she thought. *And as soon as I buy a new bathing suit.*

She walked into her apartment a few minutes later, her heart pounding from the exertion, and quickly refilled Maverick's water bowl and scooped a cup of kibble into his bowl. While he ate, she hurried down the hall to the bathroom. A glance at her watch showed her that she would have just enough time for a shower before she was due to meet the real estate agent, Madeline, at the house on Morel Street. She was eager to see what the inside of the beautiful little house looked like, but had to keep reminding herself that she likely wouldn't be able to afford it and that she shouldn't get her hopes up. *Like Madeline said, it won't hurt to look,* she thought.

A few minutes later, feeling clean and refreshed, her leg muscles pleasantly tired from the morning's jog, she said her goodbyes to Maverick and grabbed her purse, feeling optimistic as she walked out the door. It was finally time to start rebuilding her life.

She found the house easily, even though she had forgotten to write down the address. Slowing down as she eased the car along the curved driveway, she took her time to admire the thick woods between the house and the road. If she did end up living here, she would have ample privacy, that was certain. She rolled down the windows, and the smells of the forest rushed into her car. The day was overcast, and the ozone scent of looming rain seemed stronger than ever out here in the wilderness. *I wonder if it will storm later*, she thought. If so, it would mean a slow day at the deli.

Madeline was already there, parked by the house and waving as Moira came up the driveway. There was a white pickup truck parked next to her, and the deli owner worried for a moment about who it could possibly be. Was someone else here to look at the house too? Then she saw the *Maple Creek Landscaping and Yard Care* sign printed on the side of the truck and relaxed.

She turned her own car off and got out, looking around. She noticed a few things that she hadn't when she had seen the house the other day, including the sound of a softly burbling creek, and what looked like a large dog run attached to the back of the house. *Perfect for Maverick*, she thought. He would love being able to run around outside without a leash on, and she wouldn't have to worry about him wandering away if he was in a run.

Someone came around the back of the house carrying a pair of pruning shears and wearing a baseball cap pulled low over his face. He was wearing a band tee-shirt and ripped jeans. Moira waved to him, but he either didn't see her or chose to ignore her; he turned his attention to one of the bushes that had a few scraggly branches beginning to grow out.

"Hi, Moira," Madeline called to her. She strode over and shook hands with her. "That's just Ben, I thought it would be a good idea to get the yard cleaned up a bit so you can see its real potential."

"Well, it certainly looks magnificent already," Moira said. She wondered if the young man would be willing to continue with the yard work if she ended up buying the house. She certainly wouldn't have time for it herself.

"Shall we go in?" the real estate agent asked. "Or would you rather look at the yard more first?"

"Let's go in," Moira said. "I can't wait to see what the interior is like."

She followed the real estate agent up the front steps, wiping her feet on the mat just inside the door before taking in the interior. The front door opened into a hallway, with what looked like the kitchen at the other end. To her left was a beautiful sitting room with large windows that looked out into the garden. Everything was covered with a layer of dust, but Moira could imagine what it would look like after a few days of cleaning and some furniture.

She followed Madeline through the house, pausing in each room as she looked around. The office had bookshelves built into the wall, and the kitchen had an attached mudroom that opened to the fenced-in dog run. Upstairs were two large bedrooms and a gorgeous master bath. She found herself falling more and more in love with the house with each room that she entered. She had never lived so far out of town, but could see herself being happy here. The only downside would be living farther away from the deli. *But I'd be closer to Candice,* she thought.

"Can I go look around outside now?" she asked the real estate agent. "How much property does the house come with, anyway?"

"I'll have to double-check the listing to get the exact amount, but I think it's about five acres," the other woman said.

Five acres, Moira thought, amazed. It seemed like quite a bit of property to her, more than she would ever need. Living out here would be far different than even living at her old house had been; there, she had been surrounded by neighbors and houses, and the sounds of children playing, dogs barking, and the summer growl of lawn mowers. Out here it seemed like there was only birdsong and silence.

When she got outside, she noticed that Ben's truck was gone. *Probably wants to beat the rain*, she thought. She didn't blame him; the sky was beginning to look ominous.

She walked around the outside of the house, not sure what to look for, but keeping her eyes open for any obvious issues. Though the yard was a bit over-grown, the house seemed to be in good repair. The fenced-in area out back was secure, and when she finally managed to track down the sound of the creek, she was delighted to find that a little wooden footbridge had been built over it, and there seemed to be the remains of a path leading off into the forest.

She was debating whether or not to explore further when she felt the first pinpricks of rain on her face. *Time to head back to the car,* she thought. Within seconds, she could hear the soft pattering of rain on the leaves above her, and knew it was time to thank Madeline for showing her the house and go.

Her mind raced as she drove back to town, trying to figure out how she could come up with the money for the house. She knew it would be smarter to buy a smaller, more affordable house in town and put the extra money into her retirement savings, but visions of what she could do with the stone house kept returning to her. She found herself mentally decorating the interior, imagining the furniture she would buy and what colors she would paint the walls of each room.

She was so distracted by her fantasy that she almost missed her turn into the deli's parking lot, and had to brake harder than she liked to. *Keep your mind on real life,* she chided herself. She had a deli to tend to, and tomorrow, a boyfriend to see. Maybe David would be able to come up with some brilliant plan for how she could afford the house, because she was certainly drawing a blank.

"Hey, Ms. D," Darrin said when she walked in. He gave her a cheerful smile, then returned to rearranging the piles of cheese in one of the refrigerated display cases. Other than him, the deli was empty, likely thanks to the rain that was continuing to fall outside. For a moment, she thought that she even heard the low rumble of faraway thunder. "I thought you had the day off."

"I did, but I've got nothing else to do today; there's no way I'm going to the beach in this weather. I thought I'd stop in and see how things are going. How has business been?" she asked. "It wasn't too bad being here on your own?"

"It wasn't bad at all," he told her. "We had a few people early on—I think they came right after church got out—but no one since."

"I think it's supposed to storm later," she told him. "If you want, you can take off once I get the soup simmering. I doubt we'll be very busy this afternoon."

"Thanks," he told her. "I might take you up on that. I've got some reading I wanted to get done this weekend. Gotta do it before school starts up again later this month."

"Sure," she said. "I'll go start on the soup. It shouldn't take more than twenty minutes or so, so just finish up what you're doing now, and poke your head through the door to say goodbye before you go."

Humming, her thoughts still on the little house in the woods, Moira began her daily job of creating a new soup from scratch. She sliced a few cloves of garlic and tossed them in a pot to sauté with a pinch of red pepper flakes. Then she took the big bowl of cannellini beans out of the fridge and rinsed them off one last time before adding the entire thing, along with a few cups of water, to the pot where the garlic and red pepper were sautéing. The beans took a while to soak, then required attention while simmering for a couple of hours, so she was glad that she had thought far enough ahead to get them prepared the night before. *Using canned beans is certainly much easier*, she thought. *But they never taste as good.*

She then added chopped celery, olives, and chicken broth, along with nearly a cup of pesto that she had also made the previous evening. By the time Darrin opened the door to the kitchen to tell her he was leaving, the pesto bean soup was nearly finished. It was a recipe that she had recently come across and, after a few tweaks to make it unique, she was eager to see what her customers thought of it. *Though with the weather we're having today, I may end up bringing most of it home with me*, she thought.

The rain only worsened as the hours wore on. An occasional wet, bedraggled customer wandered in, but Moira's prediction of an exceptionally slow day held true. She spent the extra time cleaning until the floors and glass cases all shone, and even the bathroom smelled as fresh as spring. When she found that there were still a few hours before the deli was supposed to close, she sighed and reluctantly settled down at a bistro table with a bowl of soup, a sandwich, and a book. She knew she might as well close early, but she would feel bad if someone struggled all the way through the storm only to find that the deli was closed for the evening. Besides, there was always the chance that the weather would break and business would pick up.

She was immersed in her book so when the deli's front door slammed open and a figure in a black raincoat stepped through followed by a torrent of wind and rain, she jumped violently enough for her chair to nearly tip over. Feeling foolish, she set her book down, quickly wiped up the mess from her spilled soup, then rose to greet the customer. To her surprise, she realized that the man who had startled her so was Detective Jefferson.

"Oh, hi," she said, grabbing her dishes to take them to the kitchen. "What can I get you? I think we still have some coffee left; it's on me, if you want some."

"I'm sorry, Moira, but I'm not here for coffee." He took a deep breath. "Do you have someone to watch the deli for you?"

"Why?" she asked, her blood turning to ice at the solemn look on the man's face. "What happened?"

"There's been an incident involving your ex-husband," he told her. "We need you down at the station as soon as possible."

"Oh, my goodness," she breathed. "What happened? Is he okay? Is my daughter okay?"

"Candice is at the station right now. I'm not going to lie, it isn't good. Your ex-husband is dead, Moira."

She reeled with shock, but when she registered her daughter's name, all thoughts of keeping the deli open left her mind. Her daughter needed her, and no force on earth would keep her away from that police station.

"I'm ready," she told the detective, picking up her purse and keys and leaving the dishes, forgotten, on the counter. "Let's go.

CHAPTER FIVE

She opted to drive herself, thanking Detective Jefferson profusely for his offer of a ride, but telling him that she didn't want to impose. In truth, she wanted to use the drive to compose herself for her daughter, and she wanted the freedom to drive Candice wherever she wanted to go after they were done at the station. *Mike...* she thought. *Could it be true? Is he really dead?* She remembered her conversation with him just yesterday. He had seemed so happy, and so... well, so alive. She might not have had the best relationship with him, but she would never have wished something like this on him, or on anyone. And poor Candice. What must her daughter be going through right now? Candice had been too young to remember the loss of Moira's parents. She had never really experienced the death of someone close to her. The closest thing to that sort of loss that her daughter had lived through was when Mike had left them, but at least Candice had still been able to call and visit him.

Detective Jefferson hadn't given her any details about what had happened, and Moira couldn't keep her mind from going over the possibilities. Had Candice found him? She prayed that that wasn't the case. Her poor daughter must be beside herself right now.

She pulled into the parking lot behind Detective Jefferson, snagging her umbrella from the car's passenger side floor before hurrying into the police station. The waiting room was empty other than the secretary, who gave Moira a sad smile as she shook off her umbrella. Detective Jefferson was right behind her.

"This way," he said gently, guiding her towards the door that lead to the rest of the station. "She's in my office. I thought she might prefer the privacy."

Moira followed him, her mind still reeling with the thought of Mike, dead. What on earth had happened? Had something gone wrong with the airplane? She knew he was supposed to fly out tonight, but she didn't know when. Did the storm cause him to crash his car?

"Mom!" Candice exclaimed when Detective Jefferson let her into his office. Her daughter jumped up and hugged Moira so tightly, she had to gasp for breath.

"It's all right, sweetie. I'm here." Stroking her daughter's hair, she guided her back to the chairs by Jefferson's desk and eased her into the closest one. She took the other one and turned her green-eyed gaze to the detective.

"What happened, Detective Jefferson?" she asked, fighting to keep her voice strong. Seeing Candice like this tore her up emotionally. She couldn't even begin to imagine how she would help her daughter cope with the loss of a parent.

"I'm not certain your daughter should hear it again." He nodded at Candice. "I brought you here so she could see you. If you'd like, I'll give you a moment of privacy, then you can join me in one of the interview rooms so I can tell you what happened."

"Of course. Thank you." She waited until the detective left the room, then turned back to her daughter, who was shuddering into her hands.

"Candice, sweetheart, come here. It's okay..." She embraced her daughter again, offering tissues, trying to make sense of her daughter's hysterical words. Moira thought she caught the word "blood," and her stomach dropped. Whatever had happened didn't sound good.

When Candice was able to breathe deeply again, Moira handed her a few more tissues, leaned over to kiss the top of her head, then left the office to go find Detective Jefferson. It was time she got some answers about what had happened to Mike, and what exactly Candice had seen.

Jefferson was waiting for her in the hallway, leaning against the wall and looking tired. When he saw her, he straightened up and gestured her towards one of the more comfortable interview rooms down the hall.

"Take a seat," he said, indicating the set of plush armchairs. "I took the liberty of getting us some coffees. I'm sure you could use a boost, and I know I could."

"Thanks," she said, sitting down in one of the chairs. She held the warm mug of coffee in her hands, but didn't drink yet. She kept trying to tell herself that none of this was real, it couldn't be, but Detective Jefferson's drawn face told her otherwise.

"What happened?" she managed at last.

"This is just what I've managed to gather from your daughter and the cleaning woman at the hotel," he began. "I don't have the full story yet. Both of them were distraught, and in no place mentally for questioning." Moira nodded to show that she understood.

"About an hour ago, Candice showed up at the hotel, worried because her father had been out of contact all day. Since it was past time for him to check out of his room, a hotel maid agreed to open the room up for your daughter and see if Mike had already packed up and left." He paused. "From what she told me, up until this point your daughter's biggest concern was that her father had left without saying goodbye. She was quite upset at the idea." He paused, and Moira couldn't help but feel her heart ache for her daughter. What did it say about the sort of father Mike had been that his daughter's first thought had been that he had left without saying goodbye, not that he was hurt or in some sort of trouble?

"Go on," she said when he seemed reluctant to continue. "What happened?"

"Well, they opened up the room and found his personal items strewn all over the place; they eventually spotted Mike's body." He grimaced. "I can't tell you more than that, since it's an ongoing investigation, but I'm sure your daughter will later. It wasn't a pretty sight, and I wish she hadn't been the one to find him."

"Me too," Moira whispered, stunned. She had been expecting to hear that Mike had been in some sort of accident, not... this. Was it really possible that her ex-husband had been murdered?

"What do you need us to do now?" she asked. "Do I have to... identify the body or anything?"

"Your daughter already did that for us," he told her reluctantly. "I would never have asked her to, but she insisted." He sighed and looked away from her gaze. "I will need to ask you some questions, Moira.

Routine, since you *are* his ex-wife. I'm sure you understand."

She did, but she wasn't happy about it. All she wanted to do was comfort her daughter and try to wrap her head around the idea that the man to whom she'd been married for years was dead.

It took almost another hour for her and Candice to finish things up at the police station. Her daughter would be spending the night at Moira's apartment.

Once they got inside, she let Candice get settled in the bedroom while she boiled water for tea. She quickly made up a tray of tea, cookies, and chocolate and carried it into the bedroom to give to her daughter.

"Thanks, Mom. Can you just put it on the table?" Candice asked. "I don't feel very good right now. I just want to sleep."

"Of course, sweetheart. Come on, Maverick, let's go," Moira said to the dog curled up next to Candice on the bed. He gave Moira a mournful look and low whine when she spoke, but didn't move.

"He can stay," Candice said, reaching over to stroke the dog's soft head. "I think he knows how miserable I am right now, and he just wants to keep me company."

"Okay, just let me know if he gets annoying. I usually make him sleep on the floor, since he snores and makes the whole bed shake when he chases things in his dreams."

She let herself out of the room and shut the door behind her, hoping her daughter knew that Moira would be more than happy to get anything in the world for her. *What now?* she thought. She couldn't imagine focusing on a book or television show, but was still too shocked by everything that had happened even to think about calling her friends. *Except David,* she thought. *David needs to know.* If Mike *had* been murdered, maybe David could even be of some help in tracking down the culprit.

Disappointed when she got his voice mail, she left a quick message explaining what had happened. She told him that she would pick him up at the airport tomorrow as she had promised then hung up. *What will he think when he hears that?* she wondered. *Will he be upset that I didn't tell him about Mike being in town?* She often found herself unsure just how seriously David thought of their relationship. Did he care about her as more than just a good friend? She hoped so; she knew that the feelings she had been developing for him over the months were serious, but she was too wary of hurting their friendship to be the first to say anything.

She heard a sob from the other room and put down the phone. Now wasn't the time to figure out her relationship issues. Her daughter needed her. She also knew that she would have to explore her own emotions about Mike's death eventually. They had grown apart over the years; she had spent a long time resenting him for having an affair and leaving her and Candice, but her heart still felt heavy at the thought of him being completely gone. *If I had known, would I have done anything differently the last time I spoke to him?* she thought. Would she have taken the opportunity to tell him what she thought of him for abandoning their family, or would she have told him that she forgave him? *Is it bad that I don't know the answer to that?* she wondered as she got up to check on her daughter. She liked to think that she would have forgiven him, but when she remembered how his leaving had crushed nine-year-old Candice, she knew it wouldn't have been that simple.

CHAPTER SIX

Monday was still overcast, but at least the rain had stopped. It was unpleasantly humid, and Moira glared at her frizzy hair in the rearview mirror as she waited for David outside of the airport in Traverse City. *If only I still had my good blow dryer,* she thought. *My hair would at least be manageable.* She glanced out the window for what felt like the hundredth time and finally saw David walking towards her through the airport's automatic door.

"Thanks for picking me up," he said as he slid his luggage into the backseat. "You didn't have to, with everything else that's going on."

"Well, I promised I would," she told him. "And honestly, almost anything is better than sitting around and thinking."

"Yeah." His blue eyes were compassionate as he sat down on the passenger seat and shut the car door. He squeezed her shoulder. "How are you feeling?"

"There's no easy answer to that," she said with a groan. "My heart is breaking for Candice, and I'm scared that my ex-husband was murdered—it hits just a bit too close to home, you know? And of course I'm sad for Mike... no matter how crappy a father and husband he was, he didn't deserve to be killed."

"Have you had any definitive answer yet from the police?" David asked. "What happened?"

"I haven't heard anything yet." She sighed. "I think they're treating me like a suspect. Jefferson told me it was routine to look for motive from family members and exes first, but the more he questioned me, the more I felt him becoming suspicious."

"Try not to take it personally," he advised. "Detective Jefferson knows you well enough that he should know you're innocent. He's just trying to do his job."

"I know." She grimaced. "I hope they find Mike's killer quickly, for both my and Candice's sakes."

"I'll do whatever I can to help," he promised, laying a hand over hers. She smiled up at him, grateful beyond words for his kindness and support.

When they got back to Moira's apartment, she took Maverick out for a quick walk then told Candice they were there. Her daughter's car was still at the hotel where Mike had been found, and since the hotel was on the way to David's house, it would be easier for her to give them both a ride at the same time.

Candice appeared at the doorway to Moira's bedroom with her purse. She was no longer crying, but her eyes were still puffy and her pale face showed the lack of sleep from the night before. She greeted David in a subdued voice, then ran a hand over Maverick's head in farewell and mumbled something about going to wait in the car.

"You can keep staying here if you want, honey," Moira said.

"No, I think I'll feel better at home," she replied quietly. "I can get cleaned up, change my clothes, and spend some time down in the toy store. I need something to distract myself." Moira nodded in understanding.

"We'll be right out. Think about if you want to stop anywhere for lunch on the way there."

Once the front door was shut, she and David traded a glance. He had never had kids, but he could imagine how hard it was for her to see her normally cheerful daughter so grief stricken.

"She was the one to find him?" he asked. Moira nodded.

"She and a housekeeper at the hotel," she told him. "I would give anything to be able to go back and protect her from that."

"I know, and I'm sure she does too." David wrapped her in a quick, comforting hug before pulling the door open for her. "Let's go and see what we can do to make her feel better."

Candice, however, wasn't in the mood for cheering up. Declining their offers to take her out to eat, she insisted on going back to her apartment.

"At least let me order you a pizza," Moira insisted. "I'll pay for it over the phone, and they'll deliver it right to your door. You need to eat *something*." She was relieved when her daughter relented, and she ordered up Candice's favorite; a thick crust with bacon, pineapple, and mushrooms. She wished that there was more that she could do, but her daughter seemed adamant about having alone time, and she would have to respect that.

"Where to now?" David asked when they got back in the car.

"Well, don't you want to go home?" she asked.

"I think it's better if we talked about what we're going to do," he said. "We have a killer to catch."

"All right." She smiled at him. "You've got no idea how much your help means to me. Do you want to talk over lunch, or just go to your office?"

"Let's get takeout and then go to my office," he suggested. "I could really use some Chinese right now."

With the scents of lo mein and General Tso's chicken filling the car, Moira pulled into the small parking lot next to David's office. She was surprised by how hungry she'd become from the smell of the food. She hadn't had much of an appetite since getting the news about Mike the day before.

"I've got the drinks," he told her, grabbing the two-liter bottle of soda they'd bought. "If you get the food, I'll go unlock the door."

Even though she had known David for months, she hadn't spent nearly as much time at his office as he had spent at the deli. She looked around the welcoming space and set the food down on an end table while he scooped the pile of papers off his desk and onto a chair.

"I've got paper plates somewhere," he muttered, going into the other room to search for them. Moira sat down, taking the food out and opening the lids so the steaming noodles and chicken would have a chance to cool.

"Here we go: paper plates, napkins, and plastic cups. I forgot I had those—they must be left over from our picnic," David said a few minutes later. They dug in, eating in silence until they were full.

"So," David said, leaning back and idly using his fork to play with a noodle. "Tell me everything that happened from the second he showed up."

She relayed her afternoon and evening from the day before, trying to remember everything that Detective Jefferson had said in their conversation. It was harder than she'd thought it would be; her mind had been on Candice while the detective had been talking to her and she hardly remembered some of his questions.

"He didn't seem happy that I had no alibi for most of the day," she told David. "Other than the hour I spent with the real estate agent, and the twenty minutes or so spent with Darrin at the deli, I wasn't really around anyone for most of the day. It was a super slow day at the deli, so there aren't even any regular customers I can think of that might be able to verify that I was there after Darrin left."

"Real estate agent?" he asked, eyebrows raised. "Have you decided to sell what's left of your old house?"

"Oh, no. Though I probably will put the property on the market. I forgot to tell you—with everything else that's been happening, no wonder it slipped my mind—but I found this wonderful little stone house for sale about halfway between Maple Creek and Lake Marion," she said.

"That sounds nice. It would be the perfect place for you to live. You'd be right between the deli and Candice."

"I would love to buy it, but I think it's going to be too expensive," she admitted. "I'm still waiting on that insurance money, and since they're still investigating the fire, I don't think I can put the property on the market just yet."

"I'm sure you'll be able to figure something out," he said. "From what I've seen, you're very resourceful."

"Thanks." She gave a small smile at the compliment, then sobered as her thoughts returned to the rest of their conversation. "What do you think I should do about Detective Jefferson?"

"Just let him investigate. Don't get directly involved. I'll ask some questions, but you should stay on the fringes for this case." He drained the last of the soda in his cup, then steepled his fingers. "Let's start at the top. Can you think of anyone who would want to kill Mike?"

"No," she said. "I haven't spoken to him much over the years, and when we did talk, we kept it impersonal. I know that he lived in southern California, and worked as some sort of consultant for an insurance company. He had a girlfriend, but he told me that they'd broken up recently." She shrugged. "That's about it. Candice would know more, but I don't want to question her right now. Not until she's ready."

"Do you think the ex-girlfriend might have had motive to kill him?" David asked.

"I've got no idea. I mean, I know he can be a jerk, but even at his worst *I* never had the urge to do him in. Not seriously, anyway. Plus, his girlfriend lives in California. That's a bit far to come to kill someone, especially since he was supposed to be flying back last night."

"Matters of the heart aren't always logical," he said, resting his chin on his hand as he thought. "Anyone else that you can think of? Did he wrong any other women here in Maple Creek before he moved away?"

"No... the woman he had an affair with lives in a town about half an hour south of here. She had no idea he was married, and was very apologetic when she found out. We even had coffee once. She didn't seem like a cold-blooded killer to me." She frowned, thinking back to the horrible months when she had had to come to terms with her husband's disloyalty.

"Was he well off?" David asked, moving away from the subject of other women when he saw the look in her eyes. "Did he have fancy clothing, carry an expensive wallet, wear an expensive watch... anything that might have made him a target for a robbery?"

"Not that I can remember." She furrowed her brow, trying to remember what Mike had been wearing Saturday. "Actually, he was wearing a pretty nice watch. I suppose he makes, uh, made, a fair amount of money."

"If you can give me some personal information about him—his full name, birthdate, even his social security number if you know it—I'll do some digging and see if I can find anything promising," he said. "For all we know, he could have a criminal record a mile long or owe someone a lot of money. You never know what you'll find when you start digging into someone's life."

Moira gave him the information along with every-thing else she could remember about where he had been working the past few years. She wished now that she had paid more attention when Candice was talking about her father; any piece of information could end up being the one that would lead them to the person who had murdered her ex-husband. She could only hope that whoever had done it wasn't going to target the rest of her family next.

CHAPTER SEVEN

Over the next few days, Moira found herself more and more distracted, to the point of giving one of her regular customers the wrong order. Mike's death was frighteningly close to home, and the little information she had about what had happened just wasn't enough. She was loath to push her daughter for more details, as Candice was still understandably distraught over what had happened. She wished she could be more of a comfort to her daughter, but she didn't think her daughter felt very comfortable discussing Mike with her mother. She wasn't able to share in many of Candice's good memories of her father; over the past ten years she had been doing her best to forget her past with Mike and move forward. Discussing old times wasn't very comfortable for either of them.

"I wish Mike had never come back to visit," she grumbled to herself while scrubbing at a particularly persistent spot on one of the bistro tables. If he had just stayed in California, chances were he would still be alive.

"Here, Ms. D," Meg said from behind her, making Moira jump. "Let me do that. We're running low on soup in the back, and I don't know how to make this recipe."

"Thanks, Meg." She sighed and straightened up, feeling bad that her sour mood was even affecting her employees. None of them had been anything but helpful and supportive, even when she was distracted or short of temper. She really couldn't have asked for a better group of people to work at the deli. Even Meg, the newest employee, was fitting right in. She had started dating Dante shortly after being hired, but Moira hadn't had any complaints about their relationship affecting their work.

The soup of the day was a bit more foreign than her usual concoctions. The light, sour tamarind base stock paired with bok choy and tofu was a healthy selection, and one that tasted surprisingly good paired with the sweeter flavor of the Asian milk bread sandwich. It didn't take her long to get a new pot of the soup simmering away, but she was reluctant to go back out and deal with customers right away. *Meg could use more practice at the register anyway*, she told herself. *I might as well get a head start on the lentils.* The lentils, like the cannellini beans, would need to soak overnight to be ready for soup the next day.

After the lentils had been rinsed and poured into a pot of cool water to begin soaking, she did the few dishes that were piled next to the sink, took a couple of loaves of bread from the freezer to defrost for the sandwiches the next day, and double-checked the coming week's schedule to make sure no one was scheduled for an unfair number of hours. As Moira looked around the spotless, freshly organized kitchen and realized she couldn't find a single thing left to do, she knew she had stalled long enough. It was time to go back out and face the world.

"How can I help you?" she asked a few minutes later, back behind the counter even though she still didn't feel like herself. Her mind kept wandering, no matter how hard she tried to force herself to concentrate. *If I feel this bad, I can't even imagine how Candice must feel,* she thought.

"Um, I guess I'll have a bowl of your soup," the young man said. He was wearing a tee-shirt emblazoned with the name of some band that she thought Candice might have listened to years ago, and his hands were shoved deep into the pockets of his cargo pants. His gaze followed Meg as she helped an elderly man figure out which type of smoked turkey he had bought on his last visit to the deli. Moira thought the young man looked vaguely familiar, but couldn't make her foggy mind concentrate enough to place him. *He probably works at the grocery store or something,* she thought.

"Just a moment," she told him. "I'll go get your order."

When she came back with the soup in a to-go bowl, Meg was at the register ringing up the elderly man she had been helping. The younger man was slouched against the wall, waiting for his turn to pay. Moira handed his soup to Meg, who rang him up as soon as her first customer was done.

"Will that be cash or credit?" she asked.

"Cash, I guess." The young man pulled a wallet out of his pocket and began rummaging around inside for the correct bills. Moira, who had begun wiping down the countertop, paused, the rag dropping from her hand. On the young man's wrist was a gold watch, just like the one she had seen on Mike's wrist the day before he had died. David's words came back to her.

"Did he have fancy clothing, carry an expensive wallet, wear an expensive watch... anything that might have made him a target for a robbery?"

Was it possible that this watch, which looked so out of place on the bored young man's wrist, didn't just look like Mike's watch, but actually *was* his watch? Was she selling soup to her ex-husband's murderer?

Frozen in spot, Moira could only watch as Meg finished up the sale and the man left, soup in hand. She was mentally cursing herself for not stopping him, but what could she do? She couldn't exactly *ask* him if he was a cold-blooded killer, and if he was, then trying to detain him might put her and Meg in danger. *Oh, how I wish he had paid with a credit card,* she thought as she watched him walk away. At least with a credit card payment, she would have his name. There was no way to track someone who paid with cash.

"Are you all right, Ms. D?" Meg asked. Moira glanced over to see her employee looking at her strangely. She realized she must look quite odd, standing as if rooted to the spot and staring after her latest customer.

"I'm fine," she said, forcing a smile onto her face. "Just lost in thought. It's been a long few days. You know how it is."

She made a hurried excuse and ducked back into the kitchen, where she quickly texted David telling him what she had just seen. Her body shook in disbelief. Was it really possible that her husband's killer had just walked out of her store? Despite her shock, her mind felt clearer than it had for days. It was far better to be doing *something* to find the murderer, as opposed to just sitting around and waiting for someone else to solve the crime.

In the off chance that the young man might come back, Moira spent the rest of the day up front with Meg. She managed to greet each customer with a smile, all the while keeping her eyes peeled for the young man in the concert tee. She couldn't believe she had let him get away before; if he did come back for some reason, she vowed to come up with an excuse to find out his name, at the very least. *I wish I could remember where I've seen him before,* she thought. *If I do, I might be able to track him down.*

"Thanks for stopping by," she said a few hours later to the last customer of the day.

"You have the freshest food in town," said Beverly, the blonde woman who was renting a room from Martha. She clutched the paper bag to her chest. "I haven't even been able to find anywhere else that knows what arugula is, let alone who will make me a custom arugula and kale salad."

"If you're still going to be in town this coming weekend, you should stop by the farmers market," Moira told her with a smile. "I'm sure you'll be able to find plenty of garden-fresh fruits and veggies there. It's where I get a lot of the deli's fresh greens."

"I'm not sure how long I'll be around," the other woman admitted. "I miss home, but I'm still not done dealing with the mess my ex left behind." Her face momentarily twisted in anger, then smoothed out.

"I hope you two figure things out," she told the blonde woman. "Feel free to stop by if you ever need a sympathetic ear."

Moira watched Beverly leave, not entirely sure how she felt about the woman. She seemed nice enough, even if she did occasionally say something that made it seem as if she was disdainful of the small town. *If she's still around next week, maybe I should invite her to coffee with Martha and Denise,* Moira thought. *Denise and I both have plenty of experience with cheating husbands; she might appreciate the chance to vent.*

Deciding to talk to Martha about including Beverly in their next coffee date, Moira began the familiar task of closing the deli for the evening. She let Meg go once the kitchen was clean, and spent the last few minutes sweeping up the dining area by herself. She was glad that it was summer; in winter, when the days were shorter, night would have long since fallen. But right now, during the last weeks of August, there was still another hour or two of sunlight left after the deli closed—plenty of time for her to get back to the apartment and take Maverick to the park before settling in for the night.

She was locking the deli's front door when she felt her cell phone buzz in the pocket of her khaki capris. She pulled it out, expecting to see David's name on the caller ID, but instead saw Detective Jefferson's. Her heart skipped a beat. Had the police found out something new about Mike's death? Her keys still in the lock, she answered the phone.

"Ms. Darling, can you come down to the station?" said the familiar voice of the detective.

"I'm just closing up the deli," she told him. "I can be there in just a few minutes." She finished locking up, then paused. *Why did he call me "Ms. Darling"?* she wondered. After she had helped catch the man who had murdered his partner, the detective had become much friendlier to her, even using her first name when they ran into each other around town.

"Perfect. Thank you for being so cooperative." He hung up, leaving Moira with a bad feeling in the pit of her stomach. She walked to her car. Before she started it, she sent a second text to David. Something about the detective's voice had warned her that she might have just moved to the top of the police's list of suspects.

CHAPTER EIGHT

"Ms. Darling, I would like to introduce you to Detective Wilson, my new partner," Detective Jefferson said as he let Moira into the interview room.

"It's nice to meet you," she said to the chestnut-haired woman standing on the other side of the table. She wondered again what she was here for. Was it a good sign or a bad one that someone other than Jefferson would be talking to her?

"Please, take a seat," Detective Wilson said. She gestured to the single chair on the side of the table closest to Moira. Obediently sitting down, Moira couldn't help but glance at the small camera on the ceiling in the corner. She much preferred talking to Detective Jefferson in his office, or even in the more comfortable room used for interviewing victims. This cold, dreary room set her on edge. *Which is probably the point*, she mused.

"I have no idea why I'm here," she admitted as the two detectives sat down across from her. "Is it about Mike?"

"Yes, this is about your ex-husband," Wilson said, folding her hands neatly in front of her. "Were you aware that he had recently named you as the beneficiary on his life insurance policy?"

"What?" Moira's eyes widened. She was stunned. Why would Mike have done such a thing? Surely it must have been a mistake. He hadn't offered her a cent of financial help over the years beyond what was required by law.

"He changed his policy about two weeks ago," the female detective continued. She opened the folder in front of her. "At about the same time he bought the plane ticket for his trip out here."

"That can't be right.... He wouldn't do something like that," she told them. "Are you sure it's me that he named as beneficiary, not our daughter, Candice?"

"Here, I'll let you see for yourself." The detective pulled a paper out of the folder and slid it across the table towards the deli owner. Moira stared at the paper in shock; even with her name clearly printed on the line, she almost couldn't believe it. Then, with a sinking feeling of horror, she realized what the two detectives must think.

"I didn't know about this," she said, sliding the paper away from herself. "I swear. This is a complete shock to me."

"I'm sure it is," Wilson said, her grey eyes cold even as her voice softened. "I'm sure you understand though. We're still going to have to ask you some questions."

"Of course," Moira said. She glanced at Detective Jefferson, desperate to see even the slightest hint that he believed her, but he wouldn't meet her gaze.

"Where were you the day of your ex-husband's murder?" the woman asked.

"I went to look at a house with Madeline Frau. She's a realtor, and I'm sure she can confirm that I was there," she said. Detective Wilson glanced over at Jefferson, who nodded.

"We went over this when I questioned her before. I called the real estate company and confirmed that she did meet Ms. Frau," he told his partner.

"What did you do after that?" the female detective asked.

"I went to the deli. I didn't leave until Detective Jefferson came to get me that evening."

"Is there anyone that can confirm you were there?"

"Other than Darrin, one of my employees, no, there isn't. And, as I told Detective Jefferson last week, I sent Darrin home shortly after I got there since the weather was so bad." She sighed, racking her brain for any other alibi witness, but she couldn't think of one.

"Look," she added. "I know Mike was my ex, but we didn't hate each other. I worked hard to make sure we had a civil relationship for Candice's benefit, and I had no reason to kill him now for having had an affair ten years ago."

"No reason, other than the sizable life insurance policy that is supposed to go to you," Detective Wilson pointed out.

"I didn't know about that," Moira groaned, exasperated. "Besides, although I'm not rich, I don't exactly *need* the money. Darling's DELIcious Delights is doing pretty well, and I have—well, I had—alimony payments coming in."

"If I remember correctly, you recently lost your house in a fire, and your daughter is about to embark on a risky new business venture." Detective Wilson leaned forward and lowered her voice. "I'm sure the money from the life insurance payout would be very useful to you. I understand, Moira. You just wanted to make sure your daughter will have a good future. You were acting to benefit your little girl, weren't you?"

"I didn't do it," Moira said again, feeling near tears. "I didn't know anything about his life insurance policy, I didn't even know where he was staying until after he was killed. I wouldn't ever hurt anyone for money, let alone the father of my child."

"I think we've questioned her enough for tonight," Detective Jefferson said at last. Moira looked hopefully up at his face, but still couldn't tell if he believed her or not. Either way, she was grateful to him for stopping the interview, even if it meant she would have to come back later for more.

"Very well," Detective Wilson said reluctantly. "If you remember anything else about your where-abouts the day of your ex-husband's death, please give us a call."

Detective Jefferson walked Moira out of the building. He paused at the door to the police station and opened his mouth. For a moment, she thought he was about to apologize, but instead he shook his head.

"I'd suggest staying around town," he told her. "You know the drill. Any trips to Canada or Mexico that I should know about?"

Mutely Moira shook her head. Once the detective had disappeared back inside the building, she got into her car and leaned her temple against the warm glass of the driver's side window. It looked as if she had once again found herself the prime uspect in a murder investigation.

Even though she was exhausted and emotionally drained, she knew that she had to tell both David and Candice of the new turn that the investigation had taken. She checked the time—it was still early enough that chances were neither of them had eaten dinner yet. *I'll see if they're free; it would be nice to talk to both of them at once,* she thought.

Half an hour later, laden with two boxes of pizza, breadsticks, and a salad, she knocked on the door to Candice's apartment. Humming to herself as she waited, she fell silent when she heard raised voices coming from the soon-to-be candy shop below. *What in the world...?* She set the boxes of food down outside Candice's door and made her way back down the stairs. The back door to the candy shop was unlocked and, hesitating for only a second, she let herself in.

One of the voices she recognized immediately as Candice's, but she didn't recognize the other person's until she made her way to the main room of the candy shop and found herself face to face with an enraged Adrian.

Candice's on-again, off-again boyfriend glared at her for a moment until he realized who she was. Immediately, his face relaxed slightly and a strained smile appeared on his lips.

"Sorry, Ms. Darling. I didn't realize you were here," he said.

"What exactly is going on?" She peered around him to make sure her daughter was okay. Candice's face was red with anger, but her eyes were dry. She crossed her arms and stared at Adrian with pursed lips.

"Candice and I were just, erm... discussing... the schedule for opening the candy shop. I think it would be best to have the grand opening before kids start going back to school in September," he told her.

"And *I* told *you* that I'm going to take as much time as I need to grieve for my father," Candice snapped. Adrian raised his hands in evident surrender.

"I was just trying to help," he said.

Moira stood next to her daughter as he said goodbye and left, trying to keep her own anger from showing on her face. Who was Adrian to pressure her daughter to do anything? The candy shop was Candice's business, not his, and as far as Moira was concerned, he didn't need to be involved with it at all.

"Sorry, Mom," the young woman said once her boyfriend was gone. "Adrian told me he wanted to talk, and I didn't know it would take this long. I meant to meet you upstairs."

"It's fine, sweetie. I don't like the way he was talking to you, though," she said, following her daughter out of the candy shop and up the stairs to her apartment. "He should respect your need for space and time. Losing a parent is hard."

"He's just business minded," Candice said with a shrug. "And he *is* right. It would be better to have our grand opening before school starts again in Lake Marion. Kids will be our main customers, and if we don't open until fall or winter, we'll lose out on a lot of business."

"I think you should do what feels right to *you*." Moira bent down to grab the pizzas, then straightened up and followed her daughter into the apartment. "Take care of yourself first. You won't be able to run a business well if you're distracted."

"I want to wait until they find whoever killed Dad," Candice told her, flinching slightly as she said the words as if saying it made it more real. "But I know that could be months, or years, or even never."

Hearing her daughter talk about the murder case reminded Moira why she was there. How would Candice react when she heard that the main suspect the police had was herself? She hoped her daughter wouldn't give up hope that the killer would be caught. *Neither David nor I will rest until he's behind bars*, she thought, glad that the private investigator had already promised to help find the killer. *He'll probably be even more determined to find the real murderer now that the police are starting to look at me as a real suspect.*

A knock sounded at the door to the apartment and a moment later, as if summoned by her thoughts, David walked in. His eyes found hers immediately, and he offered her a reassuring smile. Just being around him calmed Moira and made her more certain that things would turn out all right. Grateful for the private investigator's support and friendship, she smiled back at him before opening the first box of pizza.

"Now that we're all here," she said, "let's get some food on our plates and then I'll tell you both what happened today."

CHAPTER NINE

Moira woke up bright and early the next Monday, eager at the prospect of a day off—and even more eager at the thought of what she and David had planned for the day. As she had thought, when she had told him about her interview at the police station, he had become even more determined to find the real killer as quickly as possible. His suggestion of talking to the housekeeper who had let Candice into the room where Mike had been found was a good one, though she doubted that they would discover anything that the police hadn't. Still, it was worth a try, and it was much better than sitting around and waiting for the official investigation to turn something up.

"Sorry, buddy," she said to Maverick as she fed him his breakfast. "You'll have to stay here today. It's too hot to leave you in the car, and I don't think the hotel allows dogs." She patted him on the head and tried to ignore his sad look as she gathered up her purse and keys and walked out the door without him.

David was waiting for her in the parking lot, his black car idling quietly next to hers. His windows were down, and he gave her a cheerful wave as she approached.

"I got us iced coffees," he said as she slid into the passenger seat. The morning was already hot and humid, so Moira was grateful for the sweet, cold drink. She took a sip, then pulled a small notepad out of her purse.

"I wrote down Mike's room number," she told the private detective. "So, we can check it out if we can convince one of the employees to open it up for us."

"Good. I called the hotel last night and asked what Allison Byrd's—she's the housekeeper that let Candice in—schedule is. Once I told them I was working on Mike's case, they were more than happy to tell me her hours. Luckily she has the morning shift today." He checked his watch. "She'll be at the hotel in about ten minutes. Shall we get going?"

"We might as well. The sooner Candice and I get closure, the better," Moira said.

The hotel's parking lot was nearly full when they got here. *Tourist season is still in full swing*, she thought. *But when school starts again in a couple of weeks, this place will be nearly empty.* Sometimes she envied places like Florida that were popular tourist destinations year round. No one wanted to come up to Maple Creek in the middle of winter, so for months out of every year the small shops and restaurants had to scrape by on whatever business they got from the locals. It wasn't easy, but most people found a way to make it work.

Moira followed David out of the car and through the sliding doors to the hotel's reception area. Seeing the happy tourists in their brightly colored tank tops and shorts, the teenagers glued to the glowing screens of their cell phones and the adults flipping through travel brochures, she decided the thought of a gruesome murder happening here just over a week ago was almost surreal.

"We're here to speak to Allison Byrd," David said to

the young man at the reception counter.

"I think she's upstairs, cleaning. Are you with the police?" he asked. David wordlessly took out his wallet and showed him his private investigator's identification. The young man looked impressed. "I'll page her."

While they waited for Allison to make her way down from the top floor, Moira leaned against the counter and tried to turn her thoughts away from the dire state of her life. She was soothed watching the hustle and bustle of busy people enjoying their vacations. She began to wonder about the tourists' lives. What did they do for work? What color clothes did they wear at home? How far away had they traveled for their vacations to this small town in Michigan? As she watched, her drifting thoughts returned to her own situation. She felt almost envious watching them; they seemed so carefree and happy, while she had to investigate her ex-husband's death to avoid arrest.

"Hi... are you the people that wanted to talk to me?"

Moira turned to see a young woman with light blonde hair and pale blue eyes standing nervously by the counter. She had been expecting someone older, not a girl who looked to be the same age as her daughter. She traded a glance with David.

"Are you the one who let Candice into her father's room?" she asked. The girl nodded.

"I didn't know what was... what was inside," she said, biting her lip. "I would never have done it if I had known what she would find."

"Do you mind if we ask you some questions privately?" David asked.

"Sure..." She looked over at the young man who was in charge of the reception desk, who nodded. "We can go into the break room if you want."

Hoping that they would soon get some answers, Moira followed her with David trailing behind. Maybe, just maybe, this young woman who reminded her so much of her daughter would be able to tell them something helpful. At this point, Moira would be glad of anything that would point them in the right direction.

Her thoughts flashed back to the man who had come into the deli wearing a watch identical to Mike's. When she had told David about him, he had reminded her about the security camera above the register. Disappointingly, the man had never once looked up at the camera, and the watch had been nothing more than a flash of gold as he paid Meg for the soup. With no face and no name, Moira knew even David wouldn't be able to track him down. She would just have to wait and hope that she saw him again; after all, Maple Creek was a small town. Even a murderer couldn't hide forever.

"In here," Allison said a few moments later when they reached a door at the end of a hallway. "We're right by the laundry room, so it might be a little loud, but it will at least be private."

The break room was small, but comfortable, with a couple of plush couches, a flat screen TV, and the rich scent of brewing coffee coming from a coffee maker that was still gurgling. Allison took a seat on one of the couches and gestured for David and Moira to take the other.

"What do you want to know?" she asked resignedly.

"Could you start at the beginning?" David asked. "I'm very sorry to make you go through this again, but even the smallest detail might help."

"All right." The young woman sighed. "Well, Sunday evening is usually one of our busier times, since we have so many guests checking out to go back home for work on Monday. The guest in room two-oh-nine —that girl's father—was late for check-out, but we didn't have enough people to send someone to go check on him right away. It wasn't until his daughter showed up and asked if he was still here that anyone went to his room."

"Didn't he have housekeeping service earlier that day?" David asked.

"We don't usually do housekeeping on the same day someone is due to check out. Normal check-out is at eleven, and late check-out is at three, so it doesn't really make sense to clean a room only to have to go back a few hours later to do it again," she explained.

"That makes sense," he said. "Go ahead. What happened when Candice got here?"

"Well, when she ran into me in the hallway, she told me that she had knocked on his door, but no one answered, and she was worried that he had left without saying goodbye. She wondered if I could let her into the room." Allison bit her lip nervously. "It's usually against our policy to let anyone into a room other than the guest, but since it was past his check-out time and he hadn't paid for another night, technically the room was considered empty, so I agreed to let her in."

"And what did you find?" David asked. Moira looked down, not sure she wanted to hear this part, but knowing that getting involved with the case herself might be the only way to clear her name.

"Well he was on the bed, sprawled out as if he had just fallen there." She paused and closed her eyes. "There was blood..."

"We can come back to the body," the private investigator said gently. "What about the room? Was it messy? Could you tell if anything had been stolen?"

"The room was a huge mess," she told him, obviously relieved to be able to talk about something other than the body. "It looked like someone had gone through all of the drawers, the suitcase... everything. There were clothes and papers all over the floor, and a broken bottle of wine next to the nightstand. The floor still isn't clean there."

"Do you remember if Mike... if the body had a watch on?" Moira asked, raising her gaze to the young woman's face. "It would have been gold, and looked expensive."

"I don't think he was wearing a watch," Allison told her. "But I can't be sure. Everything just happened so fast."

Moira pondered this. It was sounding more and more like Mike had been the victim of a break-in. The only odd thing was the wine. Mike had been a lot of things, but a big drinker wasn't one of them. She couldn't see him buying a bottle of wine to drink alone, and Candice wasn't old enough to drink... so who had he been drinking with?

"Thank you," David was saying. "You've been very helpful. Do you think we could see the room now?"

"Sure. I'm supposed to be figuring out how to get the wine stain out of the carpet anyway. Just let me go grab my cart, then I'll take you up there."

The room where Mike had died was stripped bare. Even the mattress was gone, leaving a lonely looking bed frame between the two nightstands. The huge, dark stain from the spilled wine was the only thing that hinted at the violence that had happened there just over a week ago. Moira had half expected the room to be just as it had been on the day of his murder, complete with blood spatters. She wondered for a moment what had happened to all of Mike's things, then realized that all of it had probably been bagged as evidence. She hoped that when the investigation was over, Candice would be able to get most of it back. Surely her daughter would appreciate her father's old things to remember him by.

"This is it," Allison told them. "The police took everything, even the mattress."

"Is the hotel going to start using this room again?" Moira asked, wondering with morbid fascination if sometime soon someone might end up staying in the very room where her ex-husband had died.

"Yeah, as soon as the new mattress gets here. I'm supposed to get the wine stain up, but if I can't, they'll have to replace the carpet." She frowned down at the stained carpet, which looked like it had already been scrubbed with a variety of cleaning agents, to no avail.

"Try getting it wet," Moira suggested. "Pour cold water on it and let it soak for a while, then rub in a paste made with baking soda and water. One it dries, vacuum it up. It may not be perfect, but it should help."

"Thanks," the young woman said, smiling gratefully at the deli owner. "I'll try that."

"I don't think we'll find anything here," David said to Moira. "It looks like the police cleaned up pretty well. Thanks again for your help, Miss." The last part was directed towards Allison, who nodded solemnly.

"I hope you find the person who did this," she told them. "Please let me know if I can be of any more help."

"I will. Here's my card in case you think of anything else." They started towards the door, but David paused mid step. Moira stopped too, following his gaze. He was staring at the hotel room's door, a frown wrinkling his brow.

"What is it?" she asked. He turned to Allison.

"Do these doors lock automatically?" he asked. She nodded. "And this one wasn't broken when you found Mike?"

"No." She shook her head. "It would take a lot to break into one of these doors. The hotel is pretty serious about security."

"Thank you," David said, his brow still furrowed. "I'll let you know if we have any more questions."

As he guided Moira gently out of the room, she tried to figure out what about the door had caught his attention. Asking him would have to wait, though—he didn't seem to want to discuss anything in front of the hotel staff. Hopefully they could find a nice, quiet booth at one of Lake Marion's restaurants, and he could tell her his theory over lunch.

On her way out of the building, she glanced a white pickup truck with the words *Maple Creek Landscaping and Yard Care* on the side. Something niggled at the back of her mind and she frowned, but then David slipped his hand into hers. When she looked over at him, he smiled.

"We'll go wherever you want for food," he said, obviously trying to cheer her up. "My treat."

"Let's drive around and see what looks good," she replied, forcing a smile onto her lips and the white truck out of her mind.

CHAPTER TEN

Their eyes were caught not by a diner, but by the Lake Marion farmers market. David parked in an adjacent lot, and they walked over to the tables, where they got grilled hot dogs, two slices of cherry pie, and some fresh blueberries. They took their food over to a secluded picnic table in the shade of a large oak tree and sat down. Moira squirted packets of ketchup and mustard on her hot dog, but was too distracted by the questions running through her head to take a bite.

"Why did you ask Allison about the door?" she asked.

"Think about it," he said, popping a blueberry into his mouth. "His hotel room wasn't broken into.

Chances are, he either knew whoever it was well enough to let them in, or the person who killed him had a room key themselves."

"You think someone at the hotel did it?" Moira said, surprised.

"I don't know, but it's a possibility. If one of the housekeepers saw his watch, or maybe expensive shoes, or electronics, she might have decided to steal from him. Maybe he walked in at the wrong time, and she panicked," he said.

Moira thought of Allison Byrd's innocent voice, and how very similar to Candice she looked with her straight, light hair. Could the young woman have had something to do with Mike's death? She doubted it, but she had been wrong before.

"What about the wine?" she asked. David raised his eyebrows, so she explained. "Mike didn't drink very much, at least not when I knew him. He'd have a beer occasionally, especially when a football game was on, but he didn't care much for wine. I can't see him buying a bottle to drink alone."

"Hmm... that does seem odd," he said. "So, you think it might have been someone he knew? Maybe a...

lady friend?" He finished the sentence awkwardly, making Moira chuckle.

"It's okay, we've been divorced for ten years. I'm fine with him seeing other women." She paused to consider his question. "I just don't know who would have it out for him. He was a friendly guy, and didn't make many enemies. Obviously my friends all had it out for him when we were going through the divorce, but I highly doubt that any of them would have *killed* him, even back then."

"You can't think of anyone at all who might have had a grudge against him?" he asked.

"No... well actually, there might be one person. But I don't think she would do something like this," Moira mused.

"Tell me about her. Does she live in Maple Creek?"

"She lives about an hour south of us," she told him. "Her name is Beth Gilliam. She was the woman that Mike had an affair with when we were still married."

"She definitely has a connection to him then, but what would her motive be?"

"Beth didn't know about me," Moira said. "And when she found out Mike was married, she was crushed. She invited me out for coffee and apologized sincerely for what had happened."

"And you think she might still be upset with Mike for what he did?"

"Maybe. She seemed to really care about him, and was pretty upset when she found out that he had been lying to her the whole time." Moira sighed and attempted to push the painful, unwanted memories of her divorce away. She had better things to think about.

"It's worth looking into," David said. He took his tiny notepad out and scribbled down the woman's name, then turned his attention to the food that was gradually cooling in front of them. "Enough of this depressing talk. Let's enjoy this beautiful day."

The day really was beautiful, with clear blue skies and a small breeze that blew away the morning's humidity. Once they had finished their meal, Moira and David strolled around the farmers market, occasionally pausing to taste a sample or purchase something that looked too delicious to pass up. The time passed slowly, and it was still before noon by the time they had finished looking at the fresh produce and homemade trinkets and returned to David's car. Once settled in the passenger seat, Moira yawned, feeling exhaustion sweep over her. *Spending so long under the hot sun sure took a lot out of me,* she thought. *I'm glad I don't have to go to the deli today; I can just go home and nap instead.*

After David dropped her off at her apartment and they said their goodbyes, Moira put the raspberries she had bought in the fridge and set the basket of heirloom tomatoes on the counter. She settled herself on the couch planning to take a nap, but sleep just wouldn't come. Try as she might, she couldn't get thoughts of the murder out of her mind. There were just too many possibilities, and no solid evidence of who had killed Mike and why. What else could she do? Who else could she question? She felt at a loss; there was nothing left to do except wait and keep her eyes peeled for the young man who had been wearing the watch that looked suspiciously like Mike's. Nothing to do... unless she was willing to question her daughter.

Moira frowned, not sure how Candice would feel at the prospect of discussing her father's death so soon. *If she seems uncomfortable, I can just change the subject,* she told herself. If her daughter *was* ready to discuss her father, then she might well be able to supply them with the missing information they needed to find the real killer.

Reluctantly, knowing that there was no other way to get the information she needed, she picked up the phone and punched in her daughter's number. A few minutes later, she and Maverick had piled into the car and were on their way back to Lake Marion to pick up Candice and drive to the beach. The coming conversation would be unpleasant, but she was determined to make the rest of the afternoon as fun for her daughter as she could.

"I'm glad we decided to do this today," Candice said, her eyes closed and her face relaxed as she reclined in the lounge chair. Twenty feet away, the Lake Michigan waves lapped at the shore. Candice, Moira, and Maverick were relaxing in the shade of the giant beach umbrella that the two women had managed to stuff in the car. The German shepherd was stretched out on one of the beach towels, his tongue hanging blissfully out of his mouth and his fur wet and sandy from his joyous run into the waves.

"Me too," her mother replied. She took a sip of water and gazed out across the lake. A few white sails were visible far out as boaters took advantage of the wonderful day. Moira took a deep breath. It was time to broach the real reason for her call to her daughter. "There's something I wanted to talk to you about..." She was interrupted by the ringing of her cell phone. She dug it out of the beach bag and recognized the deli's number. Hoping that nothing had gone wrong, she answered it.

"Hey, Ms. D, I was wondering if you were still interested in hiring someone else?" came Meg's energetic voice.

"I would like to, yeah. I probably won't advertise that we're hiring until this whole issue with my ex-husband is solved, though," Moira replied.

"Well, one of my friends is actually looking for a job. She's really nice, and is super responsible. I told her I would put in a good word with you."

"Sure, I'd be happy to give her an interview. Just tell her to bring in a résumé. Schedule her for one of the afternoons that I work this week... Maybe Wednesday?"

Shaking her head, slightly annoyed at the interruption, but glad that she might finally be getting another employee to replace Candice at the store, she turned her attention back to her daughter.

"Candice, I was wondering if I could ask you a few things... about Mike." Her daughter was silent for a moment.

"I guess," she said at last, her tone guarded. "What do you want to know?"

"Did he ever mention anyone around here that might have a reason to hurt him? You've heard a lot more about his life these last few years than I have," Moira said.

"I already thought of that, but no matter how hard I try to remember, I don't think he ever mentioned having any enemies here," her daughter told her. "I don't know why anyone would want to hurt him, anyway. He charmed people. You're like the only person he ever argued with."

"I know." Moira sighed. Mike *did* have a way with words... and with women. That's what had ended their marriage in the first place. Maybe he had wooed the wrong woman, and her husband had gotten revenge. "Do you know if he was seeing anyone while he was in town?"

"I don't know, Mom. Dad and I didn't talk about his dating life. We mostly just talked about my plans for the candy store, and me taking a trip out to California sometime next year." She fell silent, her gaze far away as she thought about the trip that would never happen now.

Frustrated, Moira dug in the sand with her toes. She didn't know what else to ask her daughter, and could sense that Candice was getting tired of talking about her father. Were there really no clues to be found about who may have killed him? An idea suddenly sprang into her head. She had saved the footage of the man wearing the watch that looked like Mike's. He had looked to be around her daughter's age, so maybe Candice would recognize him from school or around town. Digging in the beach bag, she found her phone and brought up the app that linked to the security camera.

"Watch this and tell me if you recognize anything about the guy," she said, handing the phone to her daughter. Candice watched the video, then played it a second time, leaning closer to the device and

shielding the screen from the sun with her other
hand.

"I wish I could see his face," she said with an
annoyed sigh as she handed the phone back to her
mother. "I *think* I've seen him around, but it's hard to
tell. If he would just look up for a second, I could be
certain."

"Doesn't it seem almost like he's avoiding the
camera?" Moira asked, watching the video once
again herself.

"It does," Candice agreed. "Why are you so interested in him? Do you think he had something to do
with what happened to Dad?"

"Well... maybe. He was wearing a nice gold watch
like your father wore, and when David and I talked
to Allison Byrd earlier today, she said that his watch
was missing when you and she found him."

"That's true, his watch was gone. So was his phone,"
her daughter said with a frown. "The police told me
they never found it."

"This is sounding more and more like a robbery
gone wrong," Moira said. "Maybe we should be

checking at pawn shops to see if we can recognize anything else of his. Do you know if anything else was missing?"

"I'm not sure, his room was so messy when I found him it was impossible to tell if anything had been stolen. I got the feeling that whoever went through his stuff was angry at him." Her daughter frowned at the lake, and Moira knew it was time to change the subject. She made an effort to keep the rest of their conversation positive and light, and by the time the two of them and the dog piled into the car to go home, Candice was smiling again.

CHAPTER ELEVEN

Wednesday morning coffee with her friends was a fun routine that started a few months ago. Moira, Denise, and Martha each lived very different lives, but had enough similarities that they rarely ran out of things to talk about. Moira was curious to see how Beverly would fit in with the group, and hoped that she would get a chance to learn more about the other woman. From what she knew about Martha's guest, the woman had her own share of man troubles, and she hoped that they would be able to help her at least a little.

She was the last to arrive that morning, and rushed to order her coffee before going over to the other women. Beverly was already chatting with Denise, and seemed completely at home in the social situation.

"Sorry I'm late," Moira said.

"Not a problem." Martha gestured to the empty seat next to Denise. "Go ahead and sit down. We were just talking about the Redwood Grill. Beverly wants to eat there sometime before she heads back home. Are you free any evening this week?"

"Maybe Thursday," she replied. Turning to Beverly, Moira added, "I'm glad you could come."

"Me too. It's wonderful to meet so many nice people. I'm going to have the best stories to tell when I get home." Beverly beamed.

"Be sure to tell all of your friends to come to Maple Creek next time they take a vacation," Denise said. In a quieter voice, she added, "The Grill could use the extra business."

"I thought you guys were doing well," Moira said, concerned. "You're pretty busy whenever I stop by."

"We'd be doing fine if we got this sort of business year round, but when winter hits... I just don't see how we're going to stay afloat. I guess I didn't realize just how dead this town was once snow starts falling," her friend said. "When the weather gets bad, I'm going to have to cut back on hours significantly, and maybe even let some of my employees go until spring. Last winter, we were new and benefited from curious diners, but I don't think we can count on the same crowds this winter."

"Wow, I didn't know." Moira was glad that the deli was relatively inexpensive to run, and that she and Candice could survive on the business she got from the locals during the winter. She wished there was something she could do to help her friend, but her mind was blank. The truth was, winter was hard on all of them.

"I'm so glad we never get snow where I live." Beverly shivered delicately. "Winter in Michigan sounds just terrible."

"Sometimes it's not so bad," Martha said. "Some years we hardly get any snow."

"And some years we get bucketloads," Moira added with a chuckle. "But it's not always bad. There's nothing more gorgeous than a snowy forest, and the kids love snowmobiling and sledding."

"I think I'll stick with my beaches," the blonde woman said with a laugh.

"My ex-husband lived in California," Moira said. "He always liked the warmer weather too."

"Oh, really? What's his name? I doubt I've heard of him—Cali is a big state—but you never know." She set her coffee down and cocked her head, suddenly and almost eerily focused on Moira.

"Mike Thomson," she reluctantly replied. "He passed away a little while ago." Denise patted her hand sympathetically, and Martha gave her a supportive smile. Beverly coughed and set her coffee cup down.

"I'm sorry," she gasped. "It went down the wrong pipe."

"Did you know him?" Moira asked, curious.

"I don't think so. Like I said, it's a big state. You must miss him something terrible though."

"Our relationship was... complicated," she explained. "We'd hardly spoken for ten years, then I find out he named me as the beneficiary for his life insurance a couple of weeks before he died. I have no idea why he would do that—we were hardly friends, and he was already paying alimony for the divorce. I doubt he felt like he owed me money."

"You're sure about the life insurance?" Beverly asked, her eyes narrowed.

"I didn't believe it at first, but the police showed me proof," she explained.

"I bet that makes you look pretty suspicious in their eyes."

"It does." Moira grimaced. "Can we talk about something else?"

"Of course," Martha said quickly, shooting her drama-obsessed houseguest a quelling look. "How's Maverick doing? I haven't seen him for a while."

The conversation turned away from murder, and Moira began telling her friends about her hopes for the new house, and listened as they each shared their own anecdotes. She was glad to have a break from thinking about her ex-husband, and found herself reluctant to leave the table when it was time to go back to the rest of her life, which was quite messy at the moment.

She got to the deli just in time to say goodbye to Dante, who had worked the morning shift. Meg, who'd come in an hour ago and would leave shortly before close, gave him a quick kiss goodbye as he left. Moira smiled, glad to see that the couple was still doing well. Meg's outgoing attitude was far different than Dante's shy one, but somehow their differences didn't clash, but complemented each other.

"My friend should be here in a few minutes," Meg said once Dante had left. "I know I can't guarantee her anything, but I do really think she'd be a great addition to the deli. She loves people, and is happy to work as much as you need her to." Moira stared at her employee blankly for a moment.

"The interview," she said when she remembered her hurried phone conversation with the young woman the other day. "I'm sorry. I completely forgot. I'm going to go get started on the soup; you just tell me when she gets here, all right?"

A few minutes later, Meg poked her head into the kitchen and beckoned to Moira.

"She's here," she said. "Do you want me to have her wait at one of the tables?"

"Sure. I'll be out in a second."

Once the soup was simmering and she had washed up, Moira walked out of the kitchen and glanced across the deli at her potential new employee. She was floored to see Allison Byrd, the young housekeeper who had shown her and David the room where Mike had been killed. Shocked, she glanced over at Meg to see if her employee had any idea about the connection between the two of them. The young woman just smiled and motioned with her head, oblivious to Moira's shock.

Moira approached the bistro table warily, not quite sure what to make of this coincidence. When Allison and her eyes met, they had similar looks of shock.

"Um, hi," she began. "Are you the boss?"

"I'm the owner," Moira replied. "I take it you're Meg's friend?"

"Yeah. She just told me she'd see if she could get me a job where she worked. I didn't realize you were in charge. Not that that's a problem," she added quickly, flashing Moira nervous smiled. "It's just kind of unexpected."

"I'll say." Moira sat down across the table from her and returned her smile in an effort to calm the young woman down. "It really is a small world, isn't it?" Allison nodded.

"I guess I don't have to introduce myself since you already know who I am," she said. "But here's my résumé. I do have experience in customer service, and I've got a few really good references." She slid a folder over to Moira, who took it but didn't open it.

"What about your job at the hotel? Would your hours there interfere with the hours you might be asked to work here?" she asked.

"I, uh... I got fired from the hotel," Allison admitted, looking down and blushing. "Just a few hours after you and that private detective left, actually."

"Oh." Moira had a sneaking suspicion that the young woman sitting across from her had lost her job thanks to the help that she had offered them.

"Was it because of what happened with Mike and Candice?"

"Yeah," she replied with a sigh. "It's not your fault though; the body being found there was bad publicity for the hotel, and the manager needed to fire *someone*. He wasn't even mean about it, just very matter of fact."

"I still feel responsible. You did us a huge favor and talked to us when you didn't have to," the deli owner said. *What if David and I questioning her got her in trouble?* she thought. *I might have cost this young woman her job. Besides, she's Meg's friend—I can't just leave her jobless.* "I'll take a look at your résumé, and of course I'll need your driver's license and social security card or birth certificate, but as far as I'm concerned, you're hired."

"Wow, thanks so much!" the young woman exclaimed. "I promise you won't regret it."

Moira left Allison with instructions to come back the following Monday for her first day of training, and then said goodbye. Meg stood at her shoulder, beaming as her friend waved to them both, then got in her car and pulled out of the parking lot. It wasn't until the car was turning onto Main Street that

Moira remembered what David had said. *He thought that whoever killed Mike was either someone he knew... or was someone that worked at the hotel and had a key to the room.* And she had just hired the very house-keeper that had discovered her ex-husband's body. What had she done?

CHAPTER TWELVE

She second-guessed herself plenty, but by the next day she had mostly convinced herself that Allison was innocent. Surely the police had investigated her thoroughly, and besides, she seemed more than sincere in her desire to help Moira and David with any other information that she could remember.

Moira spent her time at the deli doing finances. They weren't fun, but they had to be done, and it was reassuring to see how well the deli was doing. *Even better than last year,* she thought. She felt bad that Denise's restaurant wasn't doing so well. The other woman had just hired a second chef, and had a team of employees nearly four times the size of Moira's crew. *Her costs must be through the roof,* she thought.

Even though she knew it wouldn't help much, she resolved to start stopping by more often, even if it was just to buy a drink or an appetizer. She was meeting David later to show him the stone house that she was so in love with—maybe they could go to dinner at the Redwood Grill first. Glad that she was only working until early afternoon today, she texted the private investigator to tell him her idea, then returned her attention to the columns of numbers in front of her. The deli might have been doing well, but she was still a long way from being able to afford that house.

David picked her up at her apartment a few hours later. He patted Maverick on the head and tossed him a treat, then offered Moira his arm. She took it, feeling glad that she had decided to dress up for their date that evening. David looked handsome in his dark green shirt and black pants, and his blue eyes seemed to sparkle as he gazed at her.

"You look nice," he said as he held the car door open for her.

"Thanks," she said, ignoring the blush that rose to her cheeks. "So do you."

The Grill was only a short drive from her apartment,

and they arrived there earlier than they usually did, before the dinner rush. Since they were meeting the real estate agent in just over an hour, Moira was glad that they wouldn't have to wait long to be seated. Then she remembered her friend's predicament and immediately felt guilty. *So what if I have to wait for a little bit before they seat me if it means this place can stay in business?*

"What's wrong?" David asked as the hostess lead them to their table. Moira waited until she was out of earshot before answering; she didn't know yet if Denise's employees knew about the trouble the Redwood Grill might be facing that winter.

"Denise said the Grill might not do so well this winter," she said in a hushed voice. "She might have to cut back on hours and let some of her employees go."

"Oh, I'm sorry to hear that," David said with a grimace. "I've come to love this place. I hope your friend figures something out. If there's anything I can do to help, let me know."

"I will, but short of finding a way to stop winter from coming, I think this one is out of our hands." They paused their conversation to order drinks, then spent a few minutes looking at the menu. Moira ordered a pasta Alfredo dish with broccoli and chicken, always eager to taste food that she hadn't made herself. She realized that the Redwood Grill was one of the few places she ever ate out, unless she counted the occasional pizza with Candice.

"Something interesting happened yesterday," she began when the waitress walked away. David looked up, his expression curious, and she went on to tell him about hiring Allison Byrd at the deli.

"That was nice of you," he said. "I feel bad that she lost her job at the hotel."

"Me too. I really hope it wasn't because of anything we did," she said. "She seems really nice." She didn't mention her concerns about Allison potentially being involved with Mike's murder—they seemed too far-fetched now. She didn't need to worry him over nothing.

"How is Candice doing?" he asked.

"She's better. I think she and Adrian have been working on the toy store more. I need to stop by one of these days and see how it's coming along." She sighed. "I have to admit, I'm not too happy with the thought of that boy helping her so much. I just don't have a good feeling about him."

"Anything in particular, or just a bad vibe?" David asked her.

"Just a bad vibe. And it's just recently; when Candice was drawing up her business plan, he was amazingly helpful. But I don't like their on-again, off-again status. Lately, he's said things to upset her." She shrugged. "I'm probably just being overprotective. I know Candice can take care of herself; I just don't want to see her get hurt."

"I know." He covered her hand with his and gave her a gentle smile. "You're a good mom. I think you should trust your instincts. It won't hurt to tell her how you feel, at least."

Moira nodded; he was right. She might not be able to control everything about her daughter's life anymore, but she could still do her best to help when she could. Candice already knew she didn't like Adrian much, but there was always a chance that a calm, reasonable conversation might change her daughter's mind about her boyfriend.

She smiled back at David, who squeezed her hand once before leaning back so the waitress could put their food on the table between them.

"This is it," Moira said as they pulled into the driveway belonging to the stone house. She was surprised to find that she felt a bit nervous showing it to David. She wondered if he would like it as much as she did.

"I love the property," he said, getting out of the car and looking around at the tall trees that surrounded them on all sides. "I bet it's going to be beautiful in winter, too. You'll be able to see the stars perfectly, without any streetlights dulling the view."

"I bet you're right," she said, standing next to him and staring up at the evening sky. "Once the leaves fall, I'll have a clear view to the sky." She mentally corrected herself. *Stop talking like you're going to buy the place. You don't have the money for it—this is just looking for fun.*

A second car pulled up the driveway. Moira recognized her real estate agent's vehicle and walked over to greet her.

"Thanks for agreeing to meet me again," she said, shaking the other woman's hand. "Sorry to have you drive all the way out here so late in the day."

"No problem; I live pretty close by, and I'm always happy to help."

David introduced himself, and then Madeline led them inside, switching on the lights as she went. The house was just like Moira remembered it, and she felt an ache in her heart. Oh, how she wanted to live here.

"I can see why you like it so much," David said as they walked through the house together. "They kitchen looks like it would be great for cooking. Lots of counter space, a gas stove... it's almost three times bigger than the kitchen in your apartment."

"It also has an amazing yard for Maverick," she said. "And a spare bedroom for when Candice wants to stay the night. I would even have room to garden... though whether I would have time is another matter."

"I think it's perfect for you." He smiled over at her. "And hey, you'd be even closer to Lake Marion."

"But farther from the deli," she pointed out. "Though not by much."

"That's true. Even though it's only a few miles farther away, you'll have to deal with worse conditions in winter than you're used to. I bet it takes them a while to plow all the way out here."

"Ugh, you're right. It isn't on one of the main roads, so it will be the last priority. If we get another blizzard like we did this past winter, I might be stuck out here for days." She paused, considering. "That wouldn't necessarily be so bad, unless the power went out too."

"At least you'd have a fireplace," he pointed out. "You wouldn't freeze to death."

"True." She chuckled, envisioning herself venturing into dark and snowy woods and attempting to chop down a tree. "Though I definitely need some pointers before I trust myself with an axe."

They left a few minutes later, waving goodbye to Madeline as they drove down the driveway. Night had fallen while they were inside, and Moira was glad that it was still summer; all that talk of winter and of snow had made her cold.

When they reached her apartment, she said her goodbyes to David and made her way inside. Maverick greeted her at the door, his tail wagging a thousand miles an hour as he danced around her. Laughing at his antics, she clipped his leash on and took him outside for a short walk before bed.

While Maverick sniffed, searching for the best possible blade of grass on which to do his business, she checked her phone for messages from the deli. There was nothing, which must mean that everything had gone well. *Maybe once we get Allison trained, I can finally start taking a few days off every week,* she thought.

A wet chewing sound drew her attention away from her phone, and she glanced down to see Maverick swallow something. He put his nose to the ground to search for more of whatever it was. Moira tugged the leash back and shone her phone's flashlight at the ground, wondering what he had found that was so tasty.

She saw half of a hot dog and sighed. Her upstairs

neighbors had kids that were always throwing things off the balcony; it looked like one of them had decided to send part of their dinner flying. She just hoped that it wouldn't give Maverick indigestion. He didn't do very well with some types of people food.

"Come on, buddy, let's go in," she said. "You don't need to be eating stuff off the ground."

A few hours later she woke up to the distinctive sound of a dog vomiting. *Oh, great,* she thought as she rolled out of bed. She should have known that the hot dog wouldn't sit well with him.

She stumbled over to the light and switched it on. She glanced over to where Maverick slept on his dog bed, expecting to see the dog gazing at her with shame on his face as he always did after vomiting up something that didn't agree with him. Instead, she found him lying on his side, breathing heavily, his body visibly shaking. Next to his head was a puddle of foamy vomit, tinged pink with blood.

CHAPTER THIRTEEN

Moira rushed down the highway, disregarding the speed limit and taking her eyes off the road frequently to glance at the rearview mirror to make sure her dog was still breathing. The closest emergency vet was nearly an hour away, and all she could do was hope that Maverick would make it until they got there.

Her mind was racing as she drove. She didn't have a clue what could be wrong with him, unless the hot dog had gone bad somehow. Her poor boy was obviously suffering. He had barely been able to stagger out of the apartment, and she had had to help him into the car. His nose was dry and hot, and when she checked his gums, they were pale. She reached into the backseat several times to give his belly reassuring pats. She had no doubt that he needed a vet, and urgently, to survive. When she pulled into the emergency vet's parking lot just under an hour later, she had to run inside and ask one of the assistants to help her carry him in, because he couldn't walk. Maverick barely lifted his head as the young man scooped him up. Moira hovered beside them doing her best to comfort the distraught dog.

"Do you have any idea what happened?" the vet asked once they made it into the examination room.

"No," Moira admitted. "He ate half a hot dog off the ground earlier, but this seems worse than simple indigestion."

"It is," the vet said grimly. "I'll have to run some tests, but from his symptoms, I think he must have ingested poison of some kind. Is it okay if I take him into the back?"

Moira nodded, then collapsed on the vinyl seat in the exam room. She wished she could stay with Maverick and hoped that he wasn't scared. Taking a few deep breaths in an effort to calm herself, she picked up her phone. Even though they wouldn't be able to help, David and Candice deserved to know what was happening.

The wait seemed to take hours, but in reality the vet returned in less than twenty minutes. Grimly, he told her the prognosis.

"It appears that your dog ate some sort of poison," he said. "We'll have to start treatment immediately, and even then we won't be able to guarantee that he'll make it."

"Please, do whatever you can to save him," she begged. "Whatever it takes." The vet nodded.

"We may need to use this room for someone else, but you're free to make yourself comfortable in the waiting room," he told her. "I'll send someone out as soon as there's a change in his condition."

She settled down in one of the padded chairs in the corner of the waiting room, thankful that it appeared to be a slow night at the clinic. Only one other woman was there. She kept glancing nervously from the clock to the door that led to the back of the clinic. Moira could understand how she felt. Waiting for news about Maverick was hard.

"What kind of animal do you have?" the woman asked after a few minutes.

"I have a dog. A German shepherd," she told her, glad for the break in the silence. "How about you?"

"I've got an Irish Wolfhound. She's in surgery." The woman wrung her hands nervously. "This isn't exactly how I planned to spend my Thursday night."

"Me either." Moira sighed. "I keep racking my brain, wondering how this could have happened. Somehow Maverick got a hold of poison, but I've never used the stuff in my life."

"I saw a story on the Internet the other day about people putting things like rat poison and ground glass in pieces of meat or cheese and leaving them in dog parks," the other woman said. "Just terrible people who want to hurt animals."

Moira froze, her thoughts snapping back to the hot dog. Was it possible it had been poisoned?

"Do you know if they'll be able to do anything to help him?" she asked the woman.

"It depends on how much he ate, and how long ago he ate it," the woman said gently. "I know the vet who's on call tonight, and I'm sure he'll do everything he can to help your dog."

"You must come here a lot, then," Moira said, trying to distract herself from thoughts of Maverick. Worrying wouldn't do any good. She had to calm down and think straight if she wanted to be of any help to her dog.

"Sadly, yes. I rescue dogs, and sometimes they're in pretty bad condition," the woman said. "My name is Tamara, by the way. Tamara Hodges."

"It's nice to meet you," Moira said, reaching over to shake the other woman's hand. "I'm Moira Darling."

"Nice to meet you too, Moira." Tamara sighed, her eyes darting towards the clock again. "Sorry, I just can't help wondering what's taking so long."

"What sort of surgery is your dog having?" the deli owner asked.

"She swallowed a big piece of one of her toys, and instead of passing through, it formed a blockage. The poor girl was miserable, and couldn't eat or drink. I had to bring her in," the other woman said.

"I know she's in good hands, but I can't stop worrying about her."

"I hope she pulls through okay," Moira said. "It would be wonderful if both of us left here with happy, healthy dogs."

They fell silent after a few more minutes, both of them lost in their own thoughts. It was late, and her busy day was catching up with her. Moira yawned and felt herself slipping farther and farther into sleep. When the door on the far side of the room finally opened, she snapped awake with a start. The vet tech walked through leading the tallest dog that Moira had ever seen.

The wolfhound had wiry grey hair and soft brown eyes, and her belly was shaved. She stumbled next to the vet, but her eyes lit up when she saw her owner. Moira smiled as she watched the reunion. It was obvious that Tamara loved her dog, and the feeling was returned.

After she settled the bill, Tamara turned back to Moira. "Here," she said, wiping happy tears out of her eyes. "This is my number. If you ever want to get together for coffee to talk about dogs—or anything

—feel free to give me a call. Not every pet owner would rush out in the middle of the night to take their animal to an emergency vet, and we responsible owners have to stick together."

"Thanks," Moira said with a smile as she took the other woman's business card and offered her own in return. "I'm glad your girl is okay."

"I hope everything turns out well for you and your pooch too." Tamara waved a quick goodbye, then guided her still woozy dog out the door, leaving Moira alone in the waiting room.

It wasn't much longer before the vet came back and beckoned her over. He looked tired, but his face wasn't as grim as before. He gave her a reassuring smile as she approached.

"Well, we're out of the woods. Maverick is still a little bit out of it, and may have some lasting effects from the poison for a few days, but he should be all right."

"Oh, my goodness, thank you so much." She felt as if a huge weight had been taken off her chest. She might not have had the dog long, but he had quickly become a huge part of her life. She couldn't even imagine what it would be like to come home and not hear his nails clicking on the floor as he rushed to greet her.

"Come on in the back, and you can sit with him until he's feeling good enough to walk. Then I'll help you load him back into your car, and hopefully all of us can get some sleep before sunrise," the vet said.

Less than two hours later she was pulling into the apartment complex, exhausted but glad that the emergency had been averted. The vet bill had been hefty, but every penny was worth it. She glanced into the rearview mirror and was glad to see Maverick resting, but focusing on her and wagging his tail.

"Come on, boy, let's get inside," she said, shutting off her engine. She helped the wobbly dog out of the car and led him inside, plumping his dog bed and stroking his head before going back outside armed with a flashlight.

It only took her a few minutes to find what she was looking for: the other half of the hot dog. She picked it up and tore it in half, not surprised to see a dull green powder inside. Feeling sick to her stomach, she spent a few more minutes looking around for any other hot dog pieces, then brought what she had inside and put it in a plastic baggie. After washing her hands thoroughly, she sat on the couch and stared at the evidence. Someone had poisoned Maverick. The only question left was why.

CHAPTER FOURTEEN

Early morning sunlight streamed through the windows in Moira's kitchen, and her coffee maker gurgled away. The horror of the night before was almost surreal, and she would have imagined it was a dream if the poisoned hot dog hadn't still been waiting for her in its little baggie. Today would be busy, but the first thing she needed to do was arrange for someone to keep Maverick company while she was gone during the day.

"Poor boy," Candice said, scratching behind the dog's ears. Maverick pressed his head against her, his mouth open in a doggy grin and his tongue lolling out as he enjoyed the attention.

"You're sure it won't be any trouble for you to watch him today?" Moira asked her daughter. "I don't want to leave him alone yet, but I need to go talk to David, then work at the deli. Darrin and Dante are both out of town this evening, and I don't want Meg to have to work alone."

"Don't worry about it, Mom. I'll just hang out and watch movies here. It won't be any trouble at all. I'm just glad he's okay. Sorry I didn't get your message until this morning."

"That's fine, sweetie. I'm glad you didn't see it right away; the only thing you could have done last night was to worry. We managed just fine on our own." She bent over one last time to hug her dog, then straightened up. "All right, I should get going. The number to the local vet is on the fridge; don't hesitate to call if he seems to be acting weird. I'll keep my phone on all day too, so you can get in touch with me if something happens."

With one last glance back at her daughter and Maverick, Moira left. She double-checked to make sure that the baggie with the poisoned hot dog was in her purse, then started her car. Her first destination of the day was Lake Marion, to see if David might be able to help her track down the person that had poisoned her dog.

She pulled into the parking lot adjacent to the private investigator's office and went inside. David greeted her with a hug.

"I'm glad he's okay," he said. "What can I do to help?"

"I want to find out who left the poison for him," she said, taking the baggie with the deadly hot dog in it out of her purse and setting it on the table. "Do you have any ideas?"

"Do you think the poison was meant for him specifically, or just for any dog who happened to find it?" he asked. "Could it have been meant for another dog in your apartment complex, maybe one with a barking problem?"

"It was right outside my door," she said. "The only other dog in my building is a little white fluff-ball that only barks if someone knocks on her owner's door."

"So, you do think it was personal?"

"It seems that way." She sighed. "I don't know why anyone would want to hurt him though. He's quiet, and he's very friendly. Everyone in the building knows who he is and will come over to pet him when they see us outside."

"Maybe whoever left the poison wasn't targeting Maverick to hurt him, but because they wanted to hurt you through him," David suggested.

Moira fell silent, letting his words sink in. Was it possible that her dog had really been hurt thanks to something that she had done to make someone else angry? She immediately thought of her investigation into Mike's death. Had she gotten too close to the truth for comfort? She tried to think about who all knew that she and David were investigating. Candice did, of course, and her employees... including Allison. She felt the blood drain from her face. Had her newest employee tried to kill her dog?

"What is it?" David asked.

"I think I might have an idea about who did it," she said. "I need to make a call." He nodded and stepped away to give her privacy. Moira grabbed her cell phone, thankful that she had already added Allison's phone number to her contact list.

"Hello?" came the young woman's voice after a few rings.

"Hi Allison, this is Moira Darling, from the deli," she said. "Can you meet me there in about an hour? I thought we might get started on some training early." She felt bad about lying, but if the girl was guilty, Moira didn't want to tip her off that she suspected something.

"Oh, sorry Ms. Darling, but I can't. I'm at Cedar Point in Ohio with some friends. But don't worry, I'll be back by Monday."

"Oh." Moira paused, not sure what to think. Was it possible the girl was lying? Or if she was telling the truth, could she have set the poison out before leaving on her trip? She decided that another lie on her part might be the only way to find out. "How far away is it from Maple Creek? Candice has been talking about taking a trip there before the weather gets bad."

"It's just under a seven-hour drive. My friends and I left early Thursday morning, and we got there in time to hit a few rides before setting up in the hotel room. It's definitely worth it if you like roller coasters. Hang on, and I'll send you a picture once we hang up. Sorry again that I couldn't make it today."

Moments after she hung up, her phone buzzed and a picture of Allison and a few other girls screaming on a roller coaster came up on the screen, along with a text message.

Tell your daughter that my friends and I are planning on going again around Halloween, and she's welcome to come with us!

It seemed like the young woman was telling the truth about her trip. Moira sighed with disappointment, then chuckled at her own reaction. She should be glad that her new employee wasn't a murderer, not disappointed because it meant the real one was still out there somewhere.

"Hey, Ms. D. Candice told me what happened to your dog. I'm glad he's okay," Meg said when Moira walked into the deli a few hours later.

"Thanks," she responded. "I hope I can find out

who's responsible. Watching him be so sick was just horrible."

"Did you tell the police yet? They might be able to help. Or maybe offer a reward if someone turns the guilty person in," the young woman suggested. "When I was a kid, someone shot my mom's cat. She offered a three-hundred-dollar reward for evidence leading to the person who shot him, and the next day the guy's cousin turned him in."

"That's a great idea, Meg," Moira said, impressed. "I'll have to see what I can afford, but it would definitely be worth it to find the person responsible."

For the first few hours, an endless line of customers kept both women on their toes. Moira chatted with her customers as she rang them up, giving directions to the best beaches and recommending the ice cream parlor down the street to families that had children. She also did her best to suggest the Redwood Grill whenever she could. It felt good to know she was helping out her fellow local business owners, and it was nice to relax and enjoy the day, knowing that Maverick and Candice were safe together at her apartment.

Around three in the afternoon the lunch rush

petered out, and Moira knew from experience that the lull would last until around five. She did a quick sweep around the deli to make sure the floor was clean and everything was straightened, then pulled out her tablet and began once again to study the video of the young man who was wearing the gold watch. With Allison cleared as a suspect, this boy and the watch were the only clue that she had about what might have happened to Mike.

"What's that?" Meg asked, curious, as she passed behind Moira on her way to clean the bathroom.

"It's footage I have of a guy that came into the deli last week wearing a watch that's identical to one that Mike had," she told her employee. "It's the only lead I have, but he doesn't look at the camera once and he paid with cash, so I can't think of a way to track him."

"Let me see." Meg leaned closer to the screen. Her eyes widened when she saw herself in the video. "I remember him," she said. "He flirted with me a little bit while you were in the back."

"What's his name?" Moira asked eagerly. Could it really be this easy? She mentally kicked herself for not asking Meg about him before.

"I don't remember... Ben, or Benny, or something like that, I think. But I've seen him around town. He did the lawn care last summer at the retirement center where my grandfather lives." Meg blushed. "He always said hi to me, even then."

The deli owner stared at her, amazed that she hadn't made the connection on her own. She *had* seen the young man before – he had been the one trimming the bushes at the stone house when she had gone to look at it with Madeline Frau. Even more importantly, she remembered seeing his truck outside the hotel as well. *If he does the landscaping for them, too, then that puts him in the right place to have murdered Mike.*

Her hand shaking, Moira picked up her cell phone. She had two calls to make. With any luck at all, within just a few minutes, she would be well on the way to finding the man who had killed her ex-husband.

CHAPTER FIFTEEN

She let her car idle outside of the duplex, double-checking the address against what the real estate agent had given her. *This is it,* she thought. *This is where he lives.*

A few hours ago, she had called the hotel to ask them what landscaping service they used, in the guise of wanting to hire the same people herself. The young man at the desk had confirmed her suspicion by naming the Maple Creek Landscaping and Yard Care company. He had told her that there were a few different guys that worked for the company, and he would have to ask his boss which one was in charge of the hotel's landscaping.

Thanking him, she hung up and dialed a different number.

Her next call had been to Madeline Frau, who had been more than happy to supply her with Benjamin Hall's full name, his personal number, and even his address when Moira had mentioned how pleased she had been with the landscaping at the stone house.

"I'd love to ask him if he would continue with the work after I buy the house," she'd said, trying to sound more confident than she had felt. Luckily, Madeline was too excited by the prospect of a sale to question why Moira needed his personal number.

The only problem was, Moira wanted to be completely sure it was the right house before calling the police, and she also wanted to get another glance at that watch if she could get it. If the police responded to her call and it was the wrong person, or a different model of watch than the one Mike had, then they would laugh in her face—or, even worse, view her actions as further proof that she must be guilty. *Even if I manage to get another look at this kid's watch, it may not be enough evidence for the police to be able to do anything*, she thought. Plenty of people wore watches, and while the thought of someone who looked to be barely out of high school owning an expensive gold watch like Mike's in this neighborhood seemed absurd, it probably wouldn't be enough to convince the police he was guilty.

"I need something else," she said to herself. "Just one more piece of evidence before I make the call." With any luck, she would get that evidence sooner rather than later; she didn't want David or Candice to find out what she was doing, though she had sent David a text explaining her theory. She knew neither of them would think it was a good idea for her to stake out the duplex on her own.

It was well past dark by the time someone came out of the duplex. Moira tensed, squinting as she tried to recognize the person under the porch light. It wasn't him. She sighed. Was it possible that Madeline had given her the wrong address? Or had she punched it into her GPS wrong? There was no white truck in the driveway, but it was very possible that it was parked in the garage. *Just a little bit longer,* she thought with a sigh.

Rapping at the driver's side window made her jump. She turned and saw David standing there, his eyebrows raised. Blushing, Moira rolled down the window.

"How did you know I'd be here?" she asked.

"I didn't," he said. "I think we both had the same idea. I wanted to get a feel for this guy before turning our information over to the authorities."

"Well, it's a good thing we checked. I think we have the wrong house. I've been here for ages, and have seen people come out of both sides of the duplex, but none of them have been him."

"He could be at work, or napping, or playing video games, or any number of things," David pointed out. "I wouldn't give up hope just yet."

"Do you want to sit in here with me?" she asked him. "We could keep watch together."

"I have a better idea," he said with a grin. He pulled out his wallet and flashed her his ID. "Private investigator, remember? Most people don't know that they don't *have* to talk to me when I ask questions. Let's see if we can push that advantage now."

Glad to get out of the car, Moira locked the doors behind her and followed David across the street and up the steps to the porch. He knocked on the door, exuding a confidence that she didn't even come close to feeling. A few seconds later, an older woman answered the door.

"Hello?" she said, looking warily between the two of them.

"David Morris, private investigator," he said, showing her his identification. "Is a Benjamin Hall here? I'd like to ask him a few questions."

"Yes... that's my son. He's upstairs. Is he in some sort of trouble?" she asked, her eyes widening with concern.

"We aren't sure yet," David said. "All we want to do right now is talk." She nodded.

"Come on in. You can take a seat in the living room. Sorry it's a bit messy; we're watching my sister's niece for the weekend. Here, just shove those toys aside, and I'll be right down with Benny." She hurriedly picked up a few of the toys strewn across the living room, shooting them both an apologetic glance before disappearing up the stairs to get her son.

"I hope he didn't do it," Moira said quietly when the woman was out of earshot.

"Why?" David looked at her in surprise.

"Because she seems so nice, and it would completely crush her if her son was a murderer."

David nodded and put his hand over hers for a moment, giving it a comforting squeeze before releasing it.

"We'll find the truth, whatever it is," he said. "That's the best we can do."

They heard voices, then a few seconds later a young man came downstairs. Moira recognized him from the deli the week before, and she felt relief at the fact that they had at least found the right house. Her eyes went to his wrist, where he still wore the gold watch.

"What's going on?" Benjamin asked, looking between them sleepily. "I was taking a nap."

"We have some questions to ask you about a murder," David said. The young man's face paled.

"I didn't kill anyone," he said immediately. "Are you cops?"

"I'm a private investigator," David responded calmly. "Do you mind answering a few questions?"

"If I talk to you, does that mean I don't have to talk to the cops?" Benjamin asked warily.

"Maybe."

"Fine. What do you want to know?" he said reluctantly.

"Where did you get that watch?" Moira asked, her eyes glued to his wrist.

"This? I found it, I swear." He unclasped it and tossed it to her. "You can have it. I didn't kill no one for it, you can hook me up to a lie detector if you want. I'm telling the truth."

Her fingers shaking, Moira inspected the watch. She gasped when she saw Mike's name inscribed on the back.

"It's his," she whispered, raising her eyes to meet David's. "It's Mike's watch."

"Where did you find it?" David asked, turning to the boy, his voice hard now.

"It was just on the road, in that ditch next to the sidewalk," he mumbled. "It's not like I was stealing it, ya know?"

Moira wasn't sure she agreed with the boy's logic, but she couldn't help but be glad that he had found it. He might be able to lead them to the person who had killed Mike, or at least point them in the right direction.

"Can you show us?" she asked.

"What, now?" he asked. "It's like, almost ten."

"Do you have plans?" David asked, raising his eyebrows. The kid sighed.

"I guess not," he said. "You gotta drive, though. My truck belongs to the company I work for, and I'm not supposed to use it for personal stuff."

Ben guided them out of the neighborhood and towards a more familiar part of town. They weren't that far from Moira's old street when he had them pull the car over.

"It was around here," he said. They got out of the car and followed him down the road. He paused by a storm drain. "Yeah, right here, I think."

"Do you remember anything else?" David asked while Moira looked around. "Did you see anyone that might have dropped it?"

"No," he said. "It was dark, and still kind of wet from that huge storm. I don't think anyone else was out at all."

"All right." The private investigator sighed. "Thanks for your help. We'll give you a ride home."

Once they had dropped Benjamin off, Moira and David sat together in his car for a few minutes to try and figure out what to do next.

"Knowing where he found the watch doesn't really help us much," she said. "Anyone could have dropped it, or even thrown it out of a car window to try to get us off their trail."

"I know it isn't very comforting, but at least we know who it isn't," he pointed out. "We won't be wasting our time trying to find this guy anymore."

"I guess." Moira turned the watch around in her hands. "You should probably keep this, for now anyway," she told him. "I wouldn't want the police to find me with it. They would probably toss me in jail right away."

"I doubt they would do that, but it would definitely look incriminating," he agreed, accepting the watch.

"Did they ever interview you?" she asked, curious. "You must have been a person of interest too, since Detective Jefferson knows you and I are close. Mike was my ex-husband, after all. Jealousy is a motive, right?"

"He did call me, but I was out of town that weekend, remember?" he said. "Once I emailed him a copy of my plane and conference tickets, he was satisfied."

"That's good. I wish he would see that *I'm* innocent as well." Moira sighed. "These past two weeks have been terrible. Between Candice losing her father, me being a suspect in his murder investigation, and Maverick being poisoned... I don't even know what to expect next."

"Things will turn around," He promised her. "You should get home and get some sleep. Things will look different in the light of a new day."

CHAPTER SIXTEEN

Deciding to take David's advice a bit more literally than he had probably meant it, Moira woke up early the next morning and made her way back to the street where Benjamin had found the watch. She knew it was just a hunch, but she couldn't help feeling that there was something important about the scene that she was missing.

Her hunch turned out to be a good one. In the light of day, she recognized the road that Benjamin had directed them to the night before. It was the same road that Martha lived on, and the coincidence struck Moira strongly. Was it possible that Mike's killer was stalking her friends as well? First Maverick, and then this... she was beginning to feel certain there was a connection.

Crouching by the storm drain, Moira looked both directions, trying to determine which way was up hill. What direction had the water flowed during the storm? It was hard to tell, but she thought the road leading towards her friend's house was uphill, meaning the water would have flowed from that direction. Considering how heavy the rain had been, she had no doubt the flow could have carried the watch down to the drain, where it had likely gotten caught up on whatever branches or leaves had been there.

Did the killer intend to leave the watch in front of Martha's house as some sort of warning? she wondered. *If so, a warning for who?* She couldn't see what Martha might have to do with Mike. The other woman certainly hadn't been involved in the divorce, and she and Moira weren't even friends at the time.

Maybe I'm reading too much into this, she thought. Maybe it really was just a coincidence. She sighed and checked her phone. She had just enough time to go home and let Maverick out, then get to the deli for her shift. She could call Martha in the car and ask her if she had seen anything suspicious the night of the storm.

"Nope, nothing," her friend said. "Though if there had been someone outside my house, I doubt I would have seen them, even if they were standing right by my window. Between the wind and the rain, I couldn't see a thing. I was just glad the power didn't go out."

"Thanks. There probably wasn't anyone there," Moira said, not wanting to freak her friend out unnecessarily. "How are you doing?"

"Good. Beverly just left, and I've already got my next guest scheduled. I've just got to change the sheets and do some vacuuming, and I'll be all set." She continued talking, but Moira wasn't listening. *Beverly,* she thought. *Oh, how could I be so stupid?*

"Martha," she said, interrupting her friend. "Do you know Beverly's last name?"

"Oh, yeah... let me see..." Moira heard papers being pushed around. "It was Addison," Martha said at last. "Beverly Addison."

"Thanks." Moira hung up and dialed another number. Hopefully just the woman's name would be enough for David to go on, because if Beverly was on her way to the airport, she could be gone in a matter of hours.

It all makes sense, she thought, thrilled with the rush of solving the case as all of the clues came together. *They're both from California, first of all. And the way she acted when I talked about Mike at the coffee date was definitely suspicious. It would also explain the wine, and why he had let her into the hotel room.* Moira guessed that ex-husband would have been more than happy to let his unexpected guest in, even if he had been a bit surprised to see her. He was never one to turn away the company of a pretty woman. *But why would she want to kill him?* she wondered. *And why try to hurt my dog?*

She was so distracted by her thoughts that when a furry blur raced in front of her car as she was pulling into her apartment complex, she nearly hit it. She stomped on the brakes, and the car stopped just inches from Maverick's happy face.

"What on earth are you doing out?" she asked, hurrying to unbuckle her seatbelt and get out of the car. She breathed a sigh of relief when she managed to grab his collar before he got a chance to dash into the road. She had no idea how the dog had managed to get into so much trouble in the last few days.

"I must have left the door open," she muttered as she put him in the backseat. She was angry with herself; she shouldn't have let herself get so distracted by the case that she endangered her dog's life, and it had happened twice now. If she hadn't been looking at her phone the other night when he ate the hot dog, she might have realized what was going on and been able to stop him.

Surprisingly, her front door was closed when she pulled up to her apartment building. *Maybe someone from maintenance stopped by and Maverick slipped out,* she thought. If that was the case, she would have to call the front desk and complain. If one of their employees had accidentally let her dog out, she should have been notified immediately.

Her annoyance only increased when she dropped her keys as she was trying to unlock the door. This day just wasn't going well for her. It was with a feeling of relief that she finally got the door open, shooed the dog inside, then stepped inside herself and shut the door behind her. She turned the coffee machine's warmer on, then poured some kibble in Maverick's bowl.

"Eat quickly," she told him. "We're going to have time for a quick walk before work. We'll leave just as soon as I change my clothes."

She left him to his meal and made her way down the hallway to the bedroom. The blinds were still drawn, so she flipped on the light. It took her eyes a moment to adjust, but when she realized that there was a woman sitting on her bed, she screamed.

"Don't be ridiculous," Beverly said, calmly examining her nails. Moira's largest kitchen knife was on the bed beside her. "This isn't a horror movie. Sit down, let's talk." She patted the bed. Moira just stared.

"What are you doing here?" she managed to ask.

"What do you think? I want what's mine," the other woman said.

"Do you mean the watch?" Moira asked, her heart pounding as she tried to think of escape options.

Was there anything stopping her from just running out the way she had come?

"Oh, you found that, did you?" Beverly asked, her eyes lighting up with interest. "I wondered what happened to it. I must have dropped it somewhere."

"I found it, but I don't have it with me. I can go get it for you if you like."

"I'm not stupid," the blonde woman said, narrowing her eyes. "You're not going anywhere. And I don't want the watch anyway. It's just a trinket. I want my money."

"Your money?" Moira asked, utterly confused. "I don't have any money, and surely not any of yours."

"Oh, but you do," the woman said slyly. "Or, you will."

Suddenly Moira understood. Beverly wanted Mike's life insurance money. She remembered the woman's interest when she talked about it with Denise and Martha a few days ago, and mentally cursed herself. How could she have been so stupid? She should have kept her mouth shut.

"I don't understand," she said. "Why do you think the insurance money should be yours?" Biding for time had served her well before, hopefully it would work this time too. No matter how petite and harmless the other woman looked, she was a dangerous killer and Moira knew she had to tread carefully.

"Because I'm Mike's girlfriend, silly. We were going to get married." She sighed. "If only you hadn't come along and messed it up."

"Mike told me you two broke up a while ago," Moira said. She immediately regretted her words. The other woman's face twisted in anger.

"That's not true!" she shouted, making Moira jump. "We just had a little fight."

"If it was just a little fight, then why would you kill him?" she asked, trying to be reasonable. She hoped the other woman wouldn't notice that she was slowly backing towards the bedroom door.

"Fine, you're right." The other woman heaved a sigh and stood up, grabbing the knife casually in her right hand. Moira froze. "I killed him because the jerk left me. He was supposed to marry me, and give me the life I wanted. I figured if he didn't want to spend his life with me, I could at least get something from all the time I wasted with him." She glared at the deli owner. "The life insurance was supposed to be in *my* name. He told me he got it so I wouldn't be left with nothing if something happened to him. So that money should be *mine.*"

"You can have it," Moira promised. "If I do end up getting it, I'll give you all of it. Please, just calm down."

"I'm blonde, not an idiot," the woman said. "The second I take my eyes off of you, you're going to go running to the police, isn't that right? No, I need to make it look like *you* killed him." She pulled a piece of paper out of her pocket with the hand that wasn't holding the knife, and began to read.

"I'm drowning in guilt," she began. "I tricked Mike into naming me his beneficiary, then killed him. I can't live with it any longer. Goodbye, Candice and David. I hope you'll forgive me."

"What is that?" Moira asked, feeling sick.

"Your suicide note," Beverly said proudly. "This should fix everything."

"There's still something I don't understand," the deli owner said, beginning to panic as she saw the knife rise. She hoped she could keep the woman talking until something distracted her enough that she could make a break for it. "Why poison Maverick? Why come all the way out here to kill your boyfriend? You say you wanted his insurance money, but he changed that weeks ago."

"I didn't know," Beverly said in a choked voice. Moira was surprised to see tears in the corners of her eyes. "I thought he *loved* me. I didn't know he took my name off the insurance until you said so at the coffee shop. I didn't even realize you were his ex-wife. I was so angry when I found out... I *liked* you. You betrayed me. I wanted to poison your dog to make you feel some of what I felt." She paused, taking deep breaths. The point of the knife was shaking. "I didn't come up with the idea of faking your suicide until later."

"I'm sorry you felt betrayed," Moira said, wondering if she might talk her way out of this yet. "Look, let's just go get coffee and—ow!"

Beverly had swung the knife, leaving an inch-long gash on her forearm. Moira stumbled back into the hallway and nearly tripped over Maverick, who had finished his meal and had come to investigate the commotion.

"Don't run away from me, you deserve this!" Beverly screeched, rushing at her with surprising speed. Moira put her arm up to defend against another slash, and bit back a scream as the blade bit into her forearm a second time, this time deeper than before.

She kicked at Beverly's shin and when the woman grunted with pain she turned and fled down the hallway. She expected to feel a knife in her back at any moment, but instead heard a strangled cry. Surprised and concerned that Maverick had gotten hurt, she turned to see Beverly on the floor with the dog's teeth buried in her calf. The knife had skidded across the carpet, leaving a smeared bloodstain.

Keeping her eye on Maverick in case he let go, Moira edged her way forward until she could crouch down and pick up the knife. Then she backed up, keeping her eyes on the struggling pair until she reached the kitchen, where she quickly grabbed her cell phone and punched in the number to the police, stunned and grateful that her dog had saved her once again.

CHAPTER SEVENTEEN

Moira had never liked hospitals, so when she saw David walk into the waiting room, she wasn't surprised at the relief that had washed over her. She had had enough of the place, and the thought of her attacker resting in a bed only a few floors up made her uneasy.

"How's the arm?" he asked, walking over as soon as he spotted her.

"Better." She looked down at the swathe of white gauze that was wrapped around her forearm. "The worse of the two cuts needed stitches, and they gave me a tetanus shot and a prescription for some antibiotics. Do you have any news about Maverick?" For the last few hours, she had been worrying more about the fate of her dog than about her wounds. Even though he had only bitten someone to protect her, there was still a chance that he could be labeled dangerous and required to wear a muzzle. She was terrified at the thought that Maverick might receive a death sentence for protecting her.

"Detective Jefferson said he doesn't think there will be any issues. Maverick was perfectly friendly with him and the officers, and everyone loves him." David smiled down at her and offered her his hand. "Your dog will be fine, so now let's worry about you. Do you want to get out of here?"

"More than anything," she admitted. "Beverly is right upstairs, being treated for the bite. The officer who brought her here said she's handcuffed to the bed and someone will be posted on guard at all times, but I'd still rather be in a different building. Preferably a different state, but that might be a bit harder to achieve."

"Let's get going then," he said. "I know Candice is eager to see you."

"I hope all of this hasn't been too hard on her," Moira said, concerned. "At least Mike's killer is caught, if not exactly behind bars yet."

"I think Candice is more concerned about her mother than she is about the killer," David pointed out. "She and I are *both* very glad that you're okay."

She said her goodbyes to the emergency room staff, then followed David out to the car. Walking out of the chilly building into a bright, hot, sunny afternoon, she felt disconcerted. Although the entire encounter with Beverly had taken only a few minutes, the emergency room staff had treated her immediately, and the police were willing to postpone their interview, she felt that she'd lived several weeks in one day.

I can't believe I spent so much time around her, thought Moira with a shudder. *I had coffee with the person who murdered my ex-husband — and I didn't even realize it.* She was shaken by how normal the woman had seemed. *And if I feel this disturbed, imagine how Martha will feel when she finds out. She slept under the same roof as Beverly for almost two weeks.* She resolved to call her friend the next day to see how she was taking the news. She hoped it wouldn't discourage her friend from going ahead with the bed and breakfast idea. It would be wonderful if Martha could quit her high-stress job and manage a guesthouse full time. *Though maybe she should hire some security,* she thought. *I doubt Beverly will be the last crazy person to try to rent a room.*

As David pulled his car up to her apartment complex, she saw Candice and Maverick waiting for them outside. The dog whined happily when he saw his owner get out of the car, and Moira was glad that he didn't appear any worse for the wear. She knelt down and accepted his wet kisses as she gave him a full hug, knowing that he was why she was still alive. She rose after a moment and enveloped her daughter in another bear hug. Candice looked shaken at the sight of her bandage.

"I'm all right," she assured her daughter. "It looks worse than it is. The doctor assured me there will hardly be a scar."

"It's just so scary that I almost lost both of you," Candice said, wiping away a tear. "It really put things in perspective for me."

"I'm sorry about Mike, sweetie, I really am," Moira said as they walked into the apartment arm in arm. "You know that the two of us had our issues, but I would never have wished something like that on him."

"I know," her daughter said. "I'm glad you caught his killer. Just next time, maybe wear body armor or something." She gave a weak laugh. "Or just let the police do it."

"I'll try to remember that," Moira said with a grin, glad to see her daughter joking again. "These last few weeks haven't been fun, but at least we can start putting the pieces back together now."

"Do you know why she did it? The detective that talked to me said something about insurance, but I didn't know what she was talking about," her daughter said. "What insurance?"

"Do you want to sit down?" Moira asked. "There's something I think we should talk about."

"Sure. I'm not letting you out of my sight for the time being." The young woman took a seat at the kitchen table, then looked up at her mother. "I just want to know why all of this happened."

"Well, shortly before he flew out here to visit you, Mike named me as the beneficiary for his life insurance." She traded a glance with David. "I didn't know why he did it at first, but Detective Wilson put me in touch with his lawyer while I was at the hospital, and she explained everything. Apparently his insurance company requires that beneficiaries be over twenty-one years of age; Mike wanted to make sure that if something happened to him, you would be set, financially. He told his lawyer that he knew I would make sure you got the money if anything did happen." She paused. "Beverly, who he broke up with a few weeks ago, got it into her head that she was the legitimate beneficiary, and would get the money if she killed him. When she realized that she wouldn't be getting anything, she came after me. But that money is rightfully yours, sweetie."

"I don't want Dad's life insurance money," Candice said immediately. "It's the reason that crazy woman killed him. I don't want anything to do with it."

"You should take it, honey. It's... well, it's quite a lot of money. It would help you pay off your small business loans, plus you'd have some left over." Seeing that her daughter's stubborn expression wasn't changing, Moira sighed. "It will take a few weeks for it to come through. Promise me you'll think about it, okay?"

"I don't need to think about it," Candice said. "I don't want the money. You can keep it."

"We'll talk about this later," Moira allowed. She couldn't help but feel proud as she looked at her daughter. How many other twenty-year-olds would refuse an inheritance just because they felt it was the right thing to do?

"Fine." Candice sighed. "I'm just glad all of this is over. That woman is horrible. I hope she spends the rest of her life in jail."

Looking at her exhausted daughter who had lost a father, and her loyal dog who had almost lost his life, Moira couldn't help but agree with her daughter. Hopefully Beverly Addison would be in prison for a long, long time.

As the days passed, Moira continued to try to convince her daughter to accept the insurance money. She had been certain that once the original shock of recent events had worn off, the girl would be more willing to think about taking the money, but Candice wouldn't budge.

177

"Look," Moira said at last. "If you won't take it, I'm going to put it all in a trust fund for Maverick." She knew she was being ridiculous, but the insurance payout was going to be a lot of money, and she didn't want her daughter to miss out on her opportunity, regardless of how it had come about. The deli owner was hardly made of money, and she often worried about what would happen if something came up in Candice's life that she couldn't afford to help her with.

"You aren't going to let this go, are you?" her daughter asked with a roll of her eyes. "Fine, Mom. I'll take half, and I'll put it all towards the candy shop. It's what Dad would have wanted."

"What about the other half?" Moira asked.

"Keep it," Candice told her. "With that plus the money you're getting from the fire insurance, you should be able to buy that stone house you keep talking about."

"I couldn't—" she began, only to be cut off by her daughter.

"This is my only offer," her daughter warned. "It's either this or a trust fund for the dog." The two of them looked down at Maverick, who was laying on the ground in front of them. He seemed to sense their attention and wagged his tail lazily, thumping it against the carpet. Moira sighed.

"You win," she said, visions of new décor for the house already filling her mind. "Though I think I'll still buy something nice for Maverick." At the sound of his name, the dog lifted his head and looked up at her hopefully. The two women traded a glance, then burst out laughing.

AUTHOR'S NOTE

I'd love to hear your thoughts on my books, the storylines, and anything else that you'd like to comment on—reader feedback is very important to me. My contact information, along with some other helpful links, is listed on the next page. If you'd like to be on my list of "folks to contact" with updates, release and sales notifications, etc.... just shoot me an email and let me know. Thanks for reading!

Also...

... if you're looking for more great reads, Summer Prescott Books publishes several popular series by outstanding Cozy Mystery authors.

CONTACT SUMMER PRESCOTT
BOOKS PUBLISHING

Twitter: @summerprescott1

Bookbub: https://www.bookbub.com/authors/summer-prescott

Blog and Book Catalog: http://summerprescottbooks.com

Email: summer.prescott.cozies@gmail.com

YouTube: https://www.youtube.com/channel/UCngKNUkDdWuQ5k7-Vkfrp6A

And...be sure to check out the Summer Prescott Cozy Mysteries fan page and Summer Prescott Books Publishing Page on Facebook – let's be friends!

To download a free book, and sign up for our fun and exciting newsletter, which will give you opportunities to win prizes and swag, enter contests, and be the first to know about New Releases, click here: http://summerprescottbooks.com